P9-BJV-670

THE INFINITY CLUE

THE HARDY BOYS® MYSTERY STORIES

THE
INFINITY
CLUE

Franklin W. Dixon

Illustrated by Leslie Morrill

WANDERER BOOKS
Published by Simon & Schuster, New York

Copyright © 1981 by Stratemeyer Syndicate
All rights reserved
including the right of reproduction
in whole or in part in any form
Published by WANDERER BOOKS
A Simon & Schuster Division of
Gulf & Western Corporation
Simon & Schuster Building
1230 Avenue of the Americas
New York, New York 10020

Manufactured in the United States of America
10 9 8 7 6 5 4 3 2 1

WANDERER and colophon are trademarks of Simon & Schuster
THE HARDY BOYS is a trademark of Stratemeyer Syndicate,
registered in the United States Patent Trademark Office

Library of Congress Cataloging in Publication Data

Dixon, Franklin W.
The infinity clue.

(The Hardy boys mystery stories; 70)
Summary: The Hardy Boys solve mysteries related to
a gang of terrorists and a stolen diamond.
[1. Mystery and detective stories] I. Morrill, Leslie
H., ill. II. Title. III. Series: Dixon, Franklin W.
The Hardy boys mystery stories.
PZ7.D644In   [Fic]   81–10329
ISBN 0–671–42342–8   AACR2
ISBN 0–671–42343–6 (pbk.)
This novel is a work of fiction. Names, characters, places and
incidents are either the product of the author's imagination or are
used fictitiously, and any resemblance to actual persons, living or
dead, events or locales is entirely coincidental.

Contents

1 The Trembling Ground

Frank and Joe Hardy scanned the wide valley that appeared before them, as their yellow sports sedan rounded the crest of a hill. In the distance, a huge cylindrical tower rose from the valley floor.

"Looks like a giant barnacle," Joe remarked to his older, dark-haired brother, Frank.

Biff Hooper, a tall, muscular high school friend of the two amateur detectives, leaned forward from the backseat. "You're looking at the cooling tower. The reactor itself is in the building next to it."

Biff's uncle, Jerry Hooper, was a nuclear engineer at the Bayridge Nuclear Power Plant, located outside Bayport. He had invited the three boys on a private afternoon tour of the facility. The summer had just begun and the Hardy brothers were eager for new adventures.

A few minutes later, the yellow car arrived at the power plant's front gate, where a uniformed guard checked identifications before letting the boys pass through.

"There's Uncle Jerry," Biff said, indicating a man dressed in a white smock who stood at the entrance.

"I'm not sure you'll find this very exciting," Mr. Hooper warned as he shook Frank's and Joe's hands and led them inside. "Nuclear power is produced by a fairly simple process. No wild flashing lights or bizarre sounds like in science-fiction movies."

The group followed him along an elevated steel walkway through several levels of the immense structure.

"Is that the reactor?" Joe asked, having traced a huge pipe to its source.

"It's the tip of the iceberg, so to speak," the engineer replied. "Most of the reactor is hidden."

Frank gazed at the strange device. "Isn't a nuclear reactor like a contained nuclear bomb explosion?"

Mr. Hooper smiled. "Yes, it's similar. But it's in no danger of blowing up." He explained that water traveled through the pipes at temperatures of six hundred degrees, nearly three times the boiling temperature for water.

"Is that what's making that low rumbling noise?" Biff inquired.

"Low rumble?" his uncle asked as a look of concern crossed his face.

The group stopped and listened. A dull sound seemed to come out of the earth itself, growing by the second in intensity.

"I hear it too!" Joe cried, breaking their tense silence. "It's getting louder!"

By the time the blond youth had finished his sentence, they not only heard the rumble, but also felt the steel walkway vibrate.

Suddenly, a chorus of alarms blared warnings throughout the power plant. Fear that the whole building was about to explode gripped the young visitors, and all eyes turned to Biff's uncle for direction.

"Follow me!" Mr. Hooper frantically ordered as he went back down the steel walkway. By the time they had descended to the next level, the plant was shaking violently. Pipes began to crack, gushing huge clouds of steam. The boys stumbled and groped their way along, trying not to lose their footing.

"Watch out!" the engineer called back as a pipe broke near him.

The scalding hot steam that shot from it made the visitors' journey along the shaking steel walkway all

the more dangerous. Finally, they arrived at the control room, where men were already at work on the problem.

"Where's Joe?" Frank asked suddenly.

"He was behind me!" Biff exclaimed, as he, too, realized Joe wasn't with them.

Without hesitation, both boys ran from the control room. Although the rumbling was beginning to die down, the alarms were still blaring and the hot steam cloud cut visibility almost to zero. They called Joe's name, but the noise made by the hissing steam, the alarms, and the rumble all but drowned out their voices. To be caught by a direct spray of steam, they knew, could cook them like lobsters in a matter of seconds.

Just then, Frank stumbled over something. "Joe!" he gasped, finding his brother's body face down on the concrete floor.

Cradling the boy's limp form between them, Frank and Biff carried him through the plant toward safety. By the time they reached the control room, the rumbling had stopped. Mr. Hooper and the other engineers threw switches on the control panel, activating cut-off valves to the damaged pipes.

Frank and Biff laid Joe on a couch in the adjoining lobby. Frank could see that his brother wasn't burned, but had received a nasty lump on the head.

"Wha-what happened?" Joe asked as he slowly opened his eyes.

"You must have slipped," Frank replied, relieved that Joe was apparently all right. "Lucky for you to have landed on your thick head or you might have been hurt!"

Joe smiled thinly at Frank's kidding, but his expression became serious as Mr. Hooper approached to take a look at him. "I meant, what happened to the plant?"

All eyes turned to the nuclear engineer. His face was pale. "I'm afraid we had a minor earthquake. It seems to be over now, however, and the situation is well under control."

Frank, noticing the ashen look on Mr. Hooper's face, asked, "What might have happened if the quake had been worse?"

Mr. Hooper frowned. "The effect could have been disastrous. Had the reactor core cracked or the cooling system broken down, it could have contaminated the area for miles with radiation. Fortunately, nothing like this appears to have happened. But for safety's sake, you boys had better leave the plant immediately."

He gave them special suits to guard them against possible exposure to radiation in the plant. Now able to stand, Joe put on the suit with the help of his brother, and the three left the building. Their yellow sports sedan was still in the parking lot, unharmed by the quake. Leaving the protective suits with the guard at the front gate, the trio headed back to Bayport.

"This isn't an earthquake-prone area," observed Frank. "In fact, I've never even heard of a tremor around Bayport."

"Neither have I," Joe agreed, and switched on the radio for a broadcast on the strange event.

The earthquake, a local station reported, had affected an area about twenty miles wide, including Bayport. It registered between two and three on the Richter scale, making it a fairly small quake. Experts were, however, perplexed. No tremors had ever been recorded in the area.

"It may have been a minor quake," Joe said, feeling the lump forming above his forehead, "but this bump is anything but small!"

A worried expression came over Biff's face. "I hope everyone's okay back home!"

Frank and Joe shared Biff's concern, and they rode back to town anxious and quiet. On the way, they passed fallen telephone poles and fences. Cattle, dazed by the event, had just begun to settle down to grazing again.

By the time they reached Bayport, it was clear that the city had received much less of a jolt than the power plant. A few windows were shattered and electricity was out. A report came over the radio that the nuclear plant had been badly shaken, but the current would be restored as soon as the engineers had cleared up minor difficulties.

After dropping Biff off, Frank and Joe headed homeward.

"It could have been a lot worse," Joe remarked.

"Don't count your blessings yet," the older Hardy warned. "Earthquakes have aftershocks, sometimes as strong as the quakes themselves." He paused, then pointed to the side of the road. "Hey!" he exclaimed. "Isn't that the Mortons' car?"

A blue Ford had run off the road into a ditch. Nobody seemed to be inside.

"Looks like it," Joe answered. "Better pull over."

Chet Morton, a chunky, longtime pal of the Hardys, had often joined them in solving mysteries. He lived on a farm just outside of town.

"Do you think Chet was on his way to our place?" Joe asked, finding the vehicle unoccupied.

"He must have known we weren't home," Frank mused.

The brothers hopped back in their car. After driving a few blocks, they turned on Elm Street and parked outside their house. Night had fallen, and with the power off, homes and street lights were dark.

"Has Chet been here?" Joe asked Mrs. Hardy

14

when she greeted her sons at the door, holding a candle.

Instead of answering, she smiled. "I have a surprise for you. It's in the dining room."

Frank opened the dining room door. Seated at the table were Chet, Aunt Gertrude, Iola Morton, and Callie Shaw.

"We've been waiting hours for you two," Aunt Gertrude scolded. "Dinner is long cold!"

"Sorry," Frank apologized. "We got caught in the earthquake." He knew his aunt had a soft spot in her heart for her nephews, and that she tried to hide it behind her stern and authoritative manner.

Joe looked questioningly at Chet. "We found your parents' car."

"Don't look at me!" Chet defended himself. "She was driving." He pointed at his sister.

Pretty, pixie-faced Iola, who often dated Joe, blushed. "I guess when I felt the rumbling, I panicked."

"That clears up one mystery," Frank said with a chuckle. "But it's still a mystery to me what everyone's doing here for dinner."

"We thought we would all like to have one last meal together before we possibly never see you again," Chet said offhandedly.

"Oh, stop being so melodramatic," Mrs. Hardy said with a chuckle. Then she turned to the boys. "I

15

invited your friends to dinner when I learned about your trip to Washington, D.C."

"What trip?" Frank was dumbfounded.

His mother handed him a slip of paper. "The German ambassador called this morning with a message from your father!"

2 Unwelcome Visitors

Frank held the message up to the candlelight, read it, then passed it to his younger brother. It said:

SMITHSONIAN MUSEUM OF NATURAL HISTORY. TUESDAY ELEVEN-THIRTY. CONTACT H. W.— BEWARE INFINITY

The Smithsonian Museum of Natural History, the boys knew, was a small part of the Smithsonian Institution, a vast enterprise of scientific research and learning located in Washington, D.C.

"I wonder how this fits in with Dad's case," Joe mused.

Fenton Hardy, the boys' famous detective father, was presently in Germany investigating a ring of

17

terrorists believed to be involved in the production of sophisticated weaponry. Sponsored by the German government, Mr. Hardy's work was top secret. He couldn't even contact his own family but had to communicate through the German ambassador in Washington, Gerd Kriegler.

"The ambassador said his son, Fritz, would meet you at Washington National Airport at eleven in the morning," Mrs. Hardy told her sons as they began their candlelight dinner of roast beef and mashed potatoes.

Frank stared at his plate. "Beware infinity." He mused on his father's curious warning over the word that meant never-ending, or forever.

Joe shared his brother's concern over the cryptic note. "I wonder why Dad didn't send us more information on the case," he whispered to Frank. "He must know more about the dangers behind 'infinity' than he let on in the note. The message sounds like it was communicated to Kriegler hastily, as if Dad was in a tight spot at the time."

"I don't know," Frank answered, still appearing to be lost in thought. "Maybe Ambassador Kriegler will fill us in on the details when we get to Washington."

"I sure hope he does."

"There will be no whispering at the table," Aunt

Gertrude spoke up sternly. "If you two have something to talk about, you can either share it with all of us or save it until we've finished eating."

"We were just discussing our upcoming trip to Washington, Aunty," Frank said, not wanting to spoil the party by expressing their concern over their father.

"Actually, it's too bad you have to go," Iola spoke up. "There's a dance at the high school this weekend, and we were hoping you'd come with us."

Joe made a face. "I hate to miss it," he admitted.

Everyone talked about the dance, and the infinity clue was momentarily forgotten.

After dinner, Iola and Callie, a vivacious blonde who was Frank's girlfriend, offered to wash the dishes if the boys would do the drying and stacking. They all set to work.

"Why don't you come with us?" Joe asked Chet.

"No way," answered the chunky boy as he cleaned the dessert plate by consuming the uneaten portions. "This time you're talking about foreign terrorists, the worst kind of bad. Anyway, I want to spend a few days studying up on earthquakes."

"Too bad," Joe said as he winked at his brother, "because we'll be staying at the German Embassy, where I hear there's a European chef preparing gourmet meals every day."

"Also," Frank put in, "the Smithsonian Institution probably has an authority on seismology who would love to discuss earthquakes with you."

Chet weakened at the thought, but stood his ground. "I still say no thanks. No terrorists for me."

Frank decided not to press the point any longer, thinking it better to let Chet sleep on it and dream about great cooks serving him fantastic culinary delights. "Well, if you change your mind, we'll be flying down early in the morning."

After finishing with the dishes, Joe got some heavy rope from the garage and they all went to tow the Mortons' blue Ford from the ditch. In a few minutes, it was on the road again, and the visitors were on their way. The two sleuths returned for a good night's sleep.

"I'm still curious about that quake," Joe commented.

"I am, too," Frank agreed. "I plan to ask some questions myself when we get to Washington."

The next morning, Frank and Joe woke early and had just eaten breakfast when Chet appeared at the front door with a suitcase.

"I smell bacon," he announced, sniffing the air.

"You just missed it," Frank teased, "but we're glad you made up your mind to come along."

The phone rang and Joe picked up the receiver.

"Is this the son of Fenton Hardy?" came a male voice with a thick German accent.

"Yes," Joe answered hesitantly. "Who's this?"

"Never mind," the man went on. "I am calling to say that they have found out about your father. For your own good and for his, too, do not become involved in this matter."

There was a click, and the anonymous caller hung up.

"Who was that?" Frank asked.

"He didn't say," Joe replied, and related the message to his brother.

Frank shook his head. "If Dad's in trouble, it's important we get to the bottom of this as quickly as possible. We'd better not tell Mom, though. It may have been just a crank call and there's no point in worrying her."

The sun was well up in the sky by the time the Hardys' plane reached Washington. There the aircraft was put in a holding pattern over Washington National Airport. The pilot circled the runway for close to a quarter of an hour before getting permission to land.

Frank looked at his watch as the plane's wheels finally touched the runway with a dull thud. "We don't have too much time," he announced to his companions. The ambassador's son was supposed to meet us here fifteen minutes ago."

"I'm sure he's waiting," Joe said. "I just hope it won't take too long to get our bags."

Soon, the boys were inside the terminal building, which was crowded with rushing air travelers.

"All these people!" Chet sighed. "Do you think Fritz'll find us here?"

Just then came an announcement over the airport loudspeaker: "Frank and Joe Hardy, please come to the information desk."

"Must be Fritz," Joe remarked.

The announcement was repeated, and the boys hurried through the crowded waiting room toward the information counter. When they arrived, however, Fritz was not there, nor was anyone else except a man behind the desk.

"I'm Frank Hardy," Frank told him. "My brother and I were paged."

"Yes," the clerk nodded. "Someone left a message for you." He handed the sleuths a folded piece of paper.

FRANK AND JOE— AM BEING FOLLOWED. WAIT OUT FRONT WHILE I SHAKE HIM—FRITZ

The brothers exchanged glances. Chet was already beginning to wish that he hadn't come. They picked up their baggage and hurried toward the front entrance of the terminal building.

"He'd better shake him fast," Frank said, anxiously looking at his watch. But ten minutes passed before a small, red sports car swung up to the curb where the trio was waiting.

"Frank and Joe Hardy?" the young driver called out. He had broad shoulders, straight, blond hair, and a wide grin that never seemed to leave his face. "I'm Fritz."

Frank introduced his group to their host, who spoke English as well as the Hardys spoke German, which they had perfected on a recent case in the Rhineland.

"I'm sorry I didn't know there were three of you," Fritz apologized. "My car is not made to hold that many people."

His red sports coupe was, in fact, very small. Frank and Joe had to curl up with their chins on their knees to fit in back. Chet, for once advantaged by his large frame, got to sit up front.

"Who was following you?" Frank asked the German youth.

"I don't know." Fritz shrugged. "But he was in a dark gray Peugeot, and had been on my tail since I left the embassy. I called the airport from a pay phone to leave that message for you at the information desk. I sure didn't want to pick you up with that guy on my back. Who knows what he wanted. I finally lost him, I think." Fritz checked the rearview mirror to make sure the gray sedan wasn't behind them.

"Did you get the license number?" Frank inquired.

"I tried, but the plate was covered with mud."

"Probably on purpose," Joe put in.

"Since our government began cracking down on terrorist activities, my father has received several threats from unknown sources," Fritz told them. "We have had to be very careful."

"Especially since kidnapping has become so popular among terrorists," Joe added.

"Correct," Fritz said. "We try to vary our daily routines to make it difficult for them to attempt something like that. But let's forget about that right now. I don't even like to think about it."

Returning to his cheerful self, Fritz was anxious to talk about Frank and Joe's adventures as amateur detectives. Chet, proud to have helped solve a number of cases, related *Mystery of the Samurai Sword* to Fritz. Joe couldn't keep a grin off his face while Chet dramatically told how a reclusive Japanese business tycoon had vanished, and how the sleuths had traced his disappearance to the secret behind an ancient Japanese samurai sword. Chet's role in unraveling the mystery was greatly exaggerated, but Joe restrained himself from correcting his friend's account.

Frank, however, wasn't listening. "I hope it's not too much farther," he said, interrupting Chet's story. "We have five minutes left."

"We're almost there," Fritz replied as they passed the Lincoln Memorial and turned up Constitution Avenue.

Being early summer in the nation's capital, the grounds along Constitution Avenue were filled with tourists. Several blocks farther up, the Washington Monument jutted from a hill, and beyond that were the buildings of the Smithsonian Institution.

"We'll be passing the White House on the—" Fritz stopped short. "Oh, no!"

Traffic was slowing down in front of them, blocked by a large group of young people, many of whom were carrying protest signs. The crowd had spilled out onto the avenue in front of the White House, reducing traffic to a single line of cars.

"Looks like a demonstration of some sort," Joe said.

Motorists made their way slowly and carefully through the mob of protesters, who were shouting in chorus and waving signs. The White House, home of the President, could be seen through a high iron fence.

"What's their gripe?" Chet asked.

"Nuclear power," Frank told his friend. "An article in the news this morning said there would be a demonstration here today. That earthquake near the power plant scared a lot of people."

"I agree it wasn't any laughing matter," Joe put in as he felt the bruise he had received the day before.

He then rummaged through his bag and pulled out his camera to get a picture of the demonstration. But as he aimed the camera, one of the protesters turned toward them. With uncommon quickness, the man charged the red sports car, swinging a sign over his head.

"Watch out!" Frank cried.

Too late! The demonstrator wielded the sign like a club and jumped on the car's hood.

Smash!

3 Museum Closed

The front windshield shattered, spraying glass all over the car's occupants. Fortunately, they had had time to shield their eyes from the flying fragments. When they looked up again, the protester was already disappearing into the crowd.

"Let's get him!" yelled Joe, jumping from the car with Frank, Chet, and Fritz.

Suddenly, a large group of people rushed the car. The four boys prepared to defend themselves, even though they were hopelessly outnumbered.

"Are you guys all right?" called one youth as he ran toward them. "Is anyone hurt?"

Frank and Joe relaxed, realizing that the protesters were coming to their aid.

"We're okay," Joe said sharply, addressing the boy, who was about his age, with long, sandy hair and freckles. "But our windshield is smashed to pieces thanks to one of you. Is this supposed to be a demonstration or a riot?"

The youth's feelings were clearly hurt. "I'm sorry about what happened," he apologized. "This is a peaceful demonstration, and whoever did that wasn't one of us. What did he look like?"

Having shielded their eyes from the glass, none of the foursome had gotten a good look at the attacker.

"He must have been an old man," Chet said. "He had white hair."

Frank nodded. "I saw the white hair, but there was something else about him, something strange."

Joe held up his camera. "I tried to get a shot of him when he attacked us. I hope I caught him."

"We're late!" Frank nearly jumped when he saw the time. "It's a quarter to twelve!"

Leaving the protesters scratching their heads, the foursome climbed quickly back into Fritz's sports car and headed down Constitution Avenue toward the Smithsonian.

"It looks like someone is out to get me," Fritz said, "and whoever it is, he means business."

He stopped in front of a large stone building capped by a massive dome. "Here we are," he announced. "The Smithsonian Museum of Natural History." He deposited his passengers, and, after promising to meet them at six o'clock, drove off to shop for a new windshield.

A sign was attached to the museum's glass door. It read:

CLOSED FOR EXHIBIT CHANGES

Joe tried the door. "It's closed all right," he said in frustration.

Frank cupped his hands against the glass and peered into the dark museum. "There's a guard inside," he said.

The young detectives banged on the door and waved wildly to get the guard's attention. Finally, he got up reluctantly.

"What's the matter with you kids?" the stout little man asked, opening the door only a crack. "Can't you read? The museum's closed."

Literally sticking his foot in the door, Frank said, "We have an appointment to meet someone here at eleven-thirty."

The man looked at his watch. "Well, you're late for your date and the museum is closed all week. So I'd say you blew it." With that, he shut the door and returned to his post.

"Boy, he sure thinks he's running the show," Chet grumbled.

"And he's enjoying it," Frank added, when a pickup truck swung around the corner from behind the museum. A canvas tarp covered a load of cargo in back. Two cars full of men followed the truck, and all three vehicles turned up the avenue.

"I bet those are the guys we're supposed to see!" Joe said, angry that they had nothing to pursue the group in.

The three youths watched helplessly as the caravan of vehicles mingled with the traffic on Constitution Avenue and disappeared from sight.

"Let's check in back," Frank suggested. "There might be more where they came from."

The sleuths raced around the huge museum building where they found a small parking lot that was reserved for museum employees. To their dismay, no one else was on the way out.

Frank and Joe felt the hoods of the few cars that were left in the lot, checking to see whether the engines were still warm from recent use. None were.

"What are you doing that for?" Chet protested. "We're looking for people on their way out, not on their way in."

"That's why we're the detectives and you're not," Frank kidded his buddy. "Always look for clues, even if you're not sure what they're good for at the time. Later on, they might turn out to be valuable."

"Hey, Frank, Chet!" Joe called from the far corner of the building. "There's a basement entrance here, and it's unlocked!"

Frank and Chet hurried toward Joe. Steps led down to a door that the blond sleuth held open, and the three boys entered a dimly lit corridor.

Old museum exhibits that had been dismantled over the years were jammed into storage rooms on either side. One was filled with stuffed mammals, another with jars of pickled sea animals. "This place gives me the shivers," Chet whispered.

Near the end of the corridor, beyond an open door, was what looked like a classroom. A group of chairs were set up facing a desk and blackboard. The odor of pipe tobacco pervaded the air.

"Do you think the men were in here?" Chet asked.

"I don't know," Frank replied, "but the tobacco suggests *someone* was here recently. There are nine chairs. The same number of men were in those vehicles. I counted."

The boys started to look for clues in the makeshift classroom, hoping to get some idea who the men were and what they were up to.

"Hold it right there!" a voice suddenly shouted from behind them. Standing in the door frame, a white-haired old man held a shovel threateningly in his hands.

"It's him again!" Chet cried.

Still wary from the assault on Fritz's car less than a half hour earlier, the boys made ready to defend themselves against the white-haired man. But he didn't advance on the sleuths, he just stood guard at the door, holding the shovel like a baseball bat.

"What are you kids snoopin' around here for?" he demanded sternly.

"What are you trying to prove by threatening us with that shovel?" Joe responded with a question of his own.

"I'm planning to bring you three thieving little hoodlums to justice!" the man growled. "Now, you can either give yourselves up or we can wait like this until help comes."

"Thieving little hoodlums?" Chet cried indignantly.

"Wait a minute," Frank said, then addressed the old man. "You think we're here to burglarize the museum?"

"Of course. What else would you be doing down here?" the man sneered.

"Why did you smash our car windshield at the demonstration?" Joe took over the questioning.

"Smashed windshield? Demonstration? What in the world are you talking about? I've been here in the museum, doing my job."

"This isn't the same guy," Frank told his brother.

"There was something strange about that other one."

"You work here?" Joe asked the white-haired man.

"That's right. I'm the custodial engineer," he replied proudly. Then his expression changed. "Wait a minute, I'm the one who's asking the questions. If you kids ain't thieves, then you won't mind going to Mr. Boswell's office and explaining your business to him."

"Who's Mr. Boswell?" asked Frank.

"Museum curator," the old man replied as he stepped back into the hallway, inviting the boys out of the room.

With the custodial engineer behind them, the trio marched to the curator's office.

David Boswell was a serious but kindly looking man about their father's age. His face broke into a grin when he realized he was speaking to the sons of Fenton Hardy. "Your dad worked on a case for the Smithsonian years ago when you were toddlers. Fine man, he is."

Frank told Mr. Boswell that in fact they were following up a lead for their father.

"Well, to be honest, I'm tickled to have Fenton's sons here on a case. You'll have to forgive Jason," Boswell added, referring to the janitor. "I've given everyone working in the museum special instruc-

33

tions to be on guard against intruders. You see, we've been rearranging some things, including our mineral exhibit. That's why the museum is closed for the week. There are some very valuable stones in that display, and we don't want to take any risks, especially since the security alarm system has been temporarily disconnected. So I hope you'll understand why we're a little touchy about strangers prowling around."

Frank and Joe apologized for entering the museum without permission, but explained that under the circumstances they had no choice.

"I'll try to help you any way I can," Boswell replied, easing back into his cushioned desk chair.

Frank informed the curator of their father's cryptic message to be at the Smithsonian that day at eleven-thirty and to find someone with the initials "H. W." He also asked about the men the young detectives had seen driving from the museum.

"I can't help you on your father's note," Boswell said, knitting his brow. "There was nothing scheduled for eleven-thirty as far as I know, and the initials H. W. don't ring any bells. But I can tell you that those men were a team of geologists who use that meeting room from time to time. Their activities are supported by the museum, and it's all on the level. But if you want to know more, I can refer you to the head of the geology department."

Boswell jotted a name and office number on a slip of paper and handed it to Joe. "Ask for Professor Simmons."

The three boys found Professor Simmons's office in a far wing of the museum, but the geologist was out for a late lunch. He would be back about three.

"Now that's a good idea," Chet said. "Let's find ourselves a good place to eat."

On the way out, the boys left Joe's film at the museum's photo lab to be developed, then they strolled into the Washington Mall grounds. At one end stood the United States Capitol, and far down at the opposite end was the Lincoln Memorial, which they had passed earlier. The Washington Monument rose in the center, and large government and Smithsonian Institution buildings lined the Mall on either side. Thousands of tourists filled the area with activity.

After wandering for a while, the boys bought hot dogs and sodas from a sidewalk vendor, then sat outside the Lincoln Memorial and dangled their feet in the Reflecting Pool, a shallow, man-made lake.

"I hope the ambassador hears from Dad soon," Joe said, swishing his feet in the cool water. "I'd like to know he's okay."

"It would also give us a chance to warn him about the phone call we received," Frank added. He finished his hot dog and washed it down with one last gulp of soda. "Right now I want to hear what Professor Simmons has to say about those geologists."

A blue Frisbee sailed through the air in the direction of the sleuths. Chet, seeing that it would land in the water if he didn't catch it, got quickly to his feet.

"Watch this!" he shouted.

Just as the blue Frisbee passed over their heads, Chet leaped into the air as high as he could, which was only a few inches. He snatched at the floating disc but it sailed past them, landing out in the lake.

Kaboom! A tunnel of water shot up as the Frisbee exploded, drenching not only the three youths but several startled tourists who were walking by.

Frank and Joe looked in the direction from where the Frisbee had come. They saw a figure dart from behind some bushes and run across the Mall toward the Washington Monument.

"That's him!" Joe exclaimed, seeing the bomb thrower's white hair in the sunlight as he sped into the crowd.

4 Rent-A-Terrorist

Frank and Joe, both stars in track and field at Bayport High, took up the pursuit. Dodging tourists as if they were part of an obstacle course, the two Hardys kept the culprit in sight. But he was too fast and the boys knew he would soon be able to elude them in the crowd.

"Keep after him," Frank panted, running next to his brother. "I'll see if I can cut him off on the far side of the Monument. It's our only chance."

Joe quickened his pace, bearing off to the left in the hope it would force the assailant to veer to the right, around the Monument. Frank also stepped up his pursuit. He had learned in track to conserve energy for a final burst of speed at the end of a race.

Now he sprinted up the hill, thinking of the Washington Monument as the finish line.

At first, the plan seemed to work. The bomb thrower had arched up the hill toward the Monument where the two sleuths planned to converge. But when Frank and Joe reached the spot, the man was gone!

Exhausted, the brothers returned to the Reflecting Pool, where they found Chet wading knee-deep in the water. He had collected several pieces of blue plastic, all that remained of the Frisbee.

"You guys couldn't catch that old man?" Chet kidded as he handed over the fragments to Frank and Joe for inspection.

"We lost him in the crowd," Joe admitted.

"Hey," Frank said, examining one of the pieces, "did you notice this?"

Chet nodded. "Sure, someone drew a number eight on it, whatever that means."

"Look again." Frank turned the bomb fragment on its side.

Joe snapped his fingers. "It's the sign for infinity! This must have been what Dad was trying to warn us about!"

The symbol for infinity, ∞, looked exactly like the number eight lying on its side. The boys remembered the sign from physics class.

"Boy, I wish we had nabbed that guy," Joe said in

frustration. "That was no firecracker he heaved at us."

"And we thought it was Fritz he was after." Chet groaned.

The threesome returned to the museum and found Professor Simmons back from lunch. He was a cordial man with thick glasses, a bow tie, and buck teeth, which he showed the trio in a broad grin.

Joe went right to the point, questioning him about the team of geologists they had seen leaving the museum.

"They're doing research on the earth's crust. Why do you want to know?"

"It may be relevant to a case we're working on," Frank explained. "At this point we just want to find out something about them—who they are, what they're up to."

"Let's see," the professor said, as he folded his hands on the desk in front of him. "They came from Europe not long ago to undertake various expeditions along the Eastern Seaboard. From what I understand, they plan to research configurations in the earth's mantle, which requires that they drill a series of core samples, as well as take soundings. The team uses the museum as a kind of home base for their research. They were here this morning to pick up some equipment. You must have seen Dr. Werner on his way out."

"Dr. Werner?" Joe inquired.

"Dr. Werner heads the team. He's a well-known and respected man in his field."

"Do you know Dr. Werner's first name?" Frank asked.

"My, my, these questions are getting stranger by the minute. His first name is Hasso, Dr. Hasso Werner. Why? Have you heard of him?"

Frank and Joe exchanged quick glances. Hasso Werner could well be the "H. W." they were looking for!

"It's possible we have heard of him," Frank told the museum geologist. "How can we get in touch with Dr. Werner?"

Simmons threw up his hands. "I don't have any idea. Although we try to support his research as much as we can, we don't keep tabs on his whereabouts. I expect they were on their way to a new expedition site, although I couldn't tell you where it is. I'll be happy to call you when Dr. Werner returns, but that probably won't be for at least another week."

"I'm not sure we have that much time," Frank said in a low tone. "But I'd appreciate it if you'd let us know as soon as you hear from him."

Frank gave Simmons the German ambassador's phone number and told him they would be there for several days.

Chet had been waiting anxiously for the meeting to be over, and when it was, he took the opportunity to ask a few questions of his own.

"Do you know anything about that earthquake near Bayport?"

Simmons shrugged. "That was certainly unexpected. My only guess so far is that there may have been a weakness in the mantle that had gone undetected. Although there hasn't been any seismic activity in that area, it is possible for geological forces within the earth to build up to a sudden and unexpected rupture of the crust."

"I thought earthquakes were caused by known faults in the land," said Chet, having heard about the San Andreas fault in California.

"Most of them are," said the professor. "That's why I'm so puzzled by this one. In fact, I'm eager to get Dr. Werner's report. He's an expert on such things, and his research may give us some insight into this matter." He smiled and extended his hand to the boys. "I guess we each have our own mysteries to solve. Good luck on yours."

The three visitors thanked the professor, then headed for the photo lab, where they had left Joe's film.

"You're just in time," the operator announced as he emerged from the darkroom with wet sheets of photographic paper. He laid the prints on a table and the young sleuths gathered around.

"I got him!" Joe said, pointing to a figure caught in the act of charging. "But the color looks bad. His face is all washed out, and his eyes are . . . pinkish."

"Did you use a flash on the camera?" the darkroom operator asked Joe. "That often causes a reddish reflection off the eyes."

"No, I didn't," Joe replied, knitting his brow. Suddenly, he realized why the man's appearance seemed so strange. "There's nothing wrong with this picture," he said. "This is an albino."

Frank snapped his fingers. "That's right. It explains why he was able to run so fast. He's not an old man at all."

"You mean he really looks like that?" Chet challenged the two sleuths.

"An albino," Frank explained, "has no natural pigmentation, so his hair is white as snow. The blood vessels under his skin and in his eyes give him his only color—pink."

Chet studied the photograph for a few seconds. "Boy, he sure is a mean-looking guy."

Frank grinned. "I don't think being an albino makes you mean. But at least he'll be easy to identify if we see him again." He then checked his watch. "Fritz ought to be out front to pick us up."

"Great, I'm about ready for some of that gourmet cuisine you guys promised me," Chet said, patting his oversized tummy.

Frank and Joe looked at each other, neither one wanting to tell Chet what they had in mind for him.

"Actually, we were hoping you could do us a favor," Frank finally said. He watched his friend's expression drop to one of gloomy expectation.

"What kind of favor?" Chet asked.

"We need you for a stakeout here in the museum tonight," Joe said.

"You expect me to sit all by myself in this dark place while you two go off to the ambassador's for a big gourmet feast? Do you take me for a fool? This is your case, not mine."

Chet folded his arms and acted like the subject was closed. But secretly he was eager to help. This could be his big chance to show off his sleuthing talents.

"Look, Chet," Frank began, "Dad's message told us to be at the Smithsonian, but it didn't say whether it meant eleven-thirty in the morning or at night. We just assumed it was during the day. But now I suspect the action may be tonight, and we'd like you to keep a lookout."

"Why choose me?" Chet asked.

"Joe and I have a lot to discuss with the ambassador. If we didn't think you could handle this as well as one of us, we wouldn't ask you to do it."

"That's all I wanted to hear." Chet beamed, and agreed to keep watch in the building.

The three boys returned to Boswell's office. The curator gladly granted Chet permission to stay that evening. He gave them a key to the basement door, which would be locked for the night.

Frank and Joe then left Chet in the museum and met Fritz, who was waiting in his car out front. A short while later, they arrived at the gates of the German Embassy, which Fritz opened with a remote control switch on his dashboard.

"One of our new security gimmicks since the threats began coming in," he explained.

Inside the elegant embassy, Ambassador Kriegler greeted Frank and Joe wearing nothing but a towel around his waist. An energetic man, he gripped their hands and shook vigorously.

"Excuse me for the way I am dressed," the ambassador apologized. "I have been in the sauna. Be with you in a few minutes."

Fritz, proud of his Washington home, showed the two visitors around the building. They met Herman, the chef, who was already at work preparing dinner in the kitchen. Simmering pots and saucepans filled the room with delicious smells. Then

45

Fritz took the brothers up a winding staircase to show them his room. But before they got there, an electronic beeping signal came from a panel in the wall.

"Someone's climbed the fence," Fritz said in an anxiously hushed tone.

"Let's go," Joe commanded, pounding back down the staircase to the front door.

In a few seconds, all three boys were outside scanning the embassy yard, which was surrounded by a high fence. Upon a quick inspection of the grounds, it was clear that they were free of any intruders.

"Must have been a false alarm," Fritz deduced. "Sometimes a bird or squirrel will trigger the system. It's happened several times already and is becoming a nuisance."

Frank stood in the driveway and took one more look around. He wasn't sure at all that it had been a false alarm. Yet, the intruder clearly wasn't there now. The three youths returned inside.

The first course for dinner was a gourmet fish stew, which the ambassador ladled out into bowls for his guests. Both Frank and Joe hesitated before trying the dish, but once they had tested it, they dug in hungrily.

Frank told Ambassador Kriegler about the day's

events, and asked whether he knew anything that might aid in their investigation.

Kriegler frowned thoughtfully. "I'm expecting to hear from your father again soon. When I spoke with him yesterday, he gave me the message for you and promised to call again this evening."

"And he didn't tell you anything more than was in the message?" Frank asked.

"No." Kriegler shook his head. "I know he was on the trail of something. When he called me, he seemed anxious to relay his information and get off the line as quickly as possible. He may have been making the call at some risk of being caught. I guess he thought it was important that you boys get to the museum in time to follow up on his lead."

Kriegler paused and ladled more stew into the sleuth's bowls. A fish head ended up in Joe's, pointing straight up at him. To be polite, Joe pretended not to notice, but he suddenly lost his appetite for the delicious dish.

"As for the albino who seems to be on your trail," the ambassador continued, "he sounds to me like a man known in terrorist circles as the White Rabbit, or Rabbit for short."

Joe snapped his fingers. "Because white rabbits are albino, pink eyes and all."

Kriegler nodded. "Not only that. He is also

famous for his agility and quickness. I'm sure you learned that when you tried chasing him."

"What's his business?" Frank inquired.

"He's a bomb expert," the ambassador replied. "He once worked as a mercenary soldier in Europe. Since then, he's gone underground and hires out as a free-lance saboteur for terrorist organizations." Kriegler's expression turned grave and he spoke slowly for emphasis. "He's a very dangerous man who takes a fiendish pleasure in inventing different types of bombs, and who has little respect for human life."

Frank and Joe shuddered. "I hope Dad calls tonight," Frank said. "This Rabbit may be part of the gang he's investigating."

Kriegler frowned. "You're right. And the infinity sign may be a trademark of sorts for the Rabbit."

"An emblem suggesting that there's no end to his destruction?" Joe wondered.

"I don't know," the ambassador replied. "I'll check with my government for any further information on him."

Suddenly the same thought crossed Frank's and Joe's minds. Chet was alone in the museum right at this moment, and the Rabbit might be taking the opportunity to try a new bomb out on their best friend!

5 A Lively Dummy

The museum storage room was nearly dark. Only a light at the end of an adjoining corridor enabled Chet to see whether anyone entered through the basement door.

Chet had borrowed an American Indian costume and sat cross-legged in a museum exhibit, pretending to be one of the dummies who were grouped around a fake camp fire in front of a tepee. Earlier, this had seemed like a great idea to Chet, a perfect disguise with a good view of the hallway. But after several hours, the costume was growing uncomfortable and his legs were getting cramped.

"Maybe I'll be a lying-down Indian for a while,"

he muttered under his breath, and stretched out, putting his head on the lap of one of the dummies.

On the far side of the storage room was an Eskimo, just visible in the dim light coming from the hallway. Chet suddenly noticed that he seemed to be staring at him!

The young sleuth froze, locking his eyes on the dim figure dressed in sealskins. It moved! Chet screamed silently to himself. But when he strained to see the figure better, he could tell it remained rigid.

This is ridiculous, Chet thought; I'm playing with dummies, and I'm beginning to feel like one myself.

Next to Chet was a fake piece of meat roasting on a spit. It reminded him of how long it had been since they'd had lunch. He wasn't used to missing a meal.

Suddenly, Chet stopped breathing. The basement door at the far end of the hallway opened, then closed gently. He remained motionless as a man approached, wearing a ski mask pulled over his face. The man passed the doorway to the storage room and continued down the hall. Then his footsteps could be heard climbing a stairway to the main floor.

Chet breathed a sigh of relief. Whoever that man was, he didn't look friendly enough to tangle with.

Chet decided to wait a few minutes, then he would sneak out to call Frank and Joe. But just as he was about to leave the room, the man began to descend the stairs.

Chet quickly resumed his cross-legged position in the Indian exhibit and waited for the night visitor to pass.

Then an idea sprang into the boy's head. This might be his big chance to capture the intruder! But the thought was quickly smothered when he saw the masked figure approach in the dim light. Why should I risk my neck? he argued silently with himself. It isn't even my case.

Just then the man apparently heard a noise. He ducked into the storage room and crouched behind the door, only a few feet from the Indian display! Chet's mind went into a panic. Should he jump the man and be a hero, or should he play it safe and just watch as Frank had instructed him to do? He tried to screw up his courage to attack the masked intruder. But before he could, he heard more footsteps coming from the end of the hall. They grew louder, then stopped.

All was quiet for what seemed to Chet like an eternity. The masked figure pressed himself against the wall, waiting without a sound. Chet's body ached from the rigid position he had assumed. He scarcely dared to breathe. Then the footsteps started up again, growing softer as they went back down the hallway.

Now's my chance, Chet thought as the sounds disappeared. But before he could jump up, his stomach let out a low grumble! Startled, the masked figure swung around toward the Indian display.

Grruuup! The boy's tummy betrayed him again.

The man took a step toward him to inspect the dummies. Chet knew he had to do something, or he would be caught! He watched as the masked intruder began to look closely at the figures, touching one after the other. He seemed to be almost as scared as Chet of what would happen.

"*Wawawawawawa!*" Chet let out a piercing war whoop and sprang to his feet. Then he began dancing like an Indian warrior around the fake fire.

At this, the strange man nearly jumped out of his skin. He shrieked, turned on his heels, and fled from the room. Chet stopped his rantings as the intruder ran down the hall and out the basement door.

A second later, however, another figure appeared at the door to the room. It was a museum guard! "All right, what's going on in here?" he demanded, flipping on the light switch to reveal the young warrior standing amongst the dummies.

"I—I was just—" Chet began, but couldn't find the right words.

"You're coming with me," the guard announced and grabbed Chet by the arm.

An hour later, Frank and Joe arrived at the police station. Still in his Indian costume, Chet sat glumly on a bench in the waiting room.

"I'm glad to see you two guys!" Chet sighed. "I've never felt so stupid in my life!"

"How, Chief Sitting Fool," Joe quipped.

"Ah, cut out the jokes," Chet grumbled, "and let's get out of here."

"You're free to go?" Frank asked.

"Sure. They called Boswell's house and got the whole story. I tried explaining everything to that museum guard before he dragged me here, but he was so gung ho about his job, I couldn't get through to him."

"What about that guy you saw in the museum?" Joe questioned. "Can you describe him at all?"

"Just that he was medium height, medium build. He wasn't the man who attacked us."

"We know who that albino is," Frank explained. He related the ambassador's story as they returned to the red sports car, which Fritz had let them borrow.

"Wow, he sounds too dangerous for me!" Chet remarked with a shiver as he sank into the front seat.

"We also called Sam," Joe spoke up, referring to Sam Radley, a detective who often assisted Mr.

Hardy on cases. "He's going to dig up what he can about Dr. Werner."

"What about your dad? Has he been in touch with the ambassador today?" Chet asked.

"He was supposed to call, but never did," Frank replied, his tone hiding his worry. "Must have been too busy to make it to a phone."

For a while, the three boys rode through the streets of the nation's capital in silence.

"Hey!" Chet blurted as his foot hit something crinkly. He bent down to pull a brown paper bag from beneath the seat. He opened it and his eyes lit up. "It's a can of food, and am I ever hungry!" Then he realized there was no can opener, so he sat back in his seat with a groan.

"Let me see that," Frank said anxiously. He reached over and grabbed the can from Chet. Examining it closely, he found a small figure etched in the bottom of the can. "It's the infinity sign!" he shouted, and instantly hurled the object out the window.

The can rolled into a sewer. A moment later, they heard a muffled explosion and saw a flash of flames shoot from the sewer drain.

"That was too close for comfort!" Chet breathed, wild-eyed.

"I bet the Rabbit planted that thing at the embassy," Joe growled. "He must've got in and out

54

of the premises so fast that we thought the alarm had gone off by accident."

"That man's becoming a real menace," Chet put in, now more angered than stunned. "I wonder how he knew we'd all be in here when the bomb was set to go off."

"He didn't," Frank spoke up. "There must have been a radio controlled detonator that the Rabbit could set off when just the right people were in the car."

When the trio returned to the embassy, they told their story to Fritz and the ambassador. As a result, Kriegler had several security guards placed around the embassy.

In the morning, the boys sat down to a continental breakfast, which was no more than a cup of coffee and pastry.

"This isn't much to go on," Chet whispered to Frank and Joe.

"Come with me," Fritz said, noticing the chubby boy's dismay over the light meal. "We'll go out to the kitchen and rustle up some real grub, as you Americans say."

Chet followed Fritz in search of ham and eggs, while the Hardys discussed their plans.

"I'd like to go back to that meeting room the geologists were using," Joe said. "We didn't really have a chance to search it thoroughly yesterday."

"Good idea," Frank agreed. "I also wonder what that masked guy was doing in the museum last night. It certainly wasn't any ordinary business!"

After breakfast, Frank, Joe, and Chet returned to the Smithsonian in Fritz's car, having searched it for bombs before leaving. They unlocked the basement door with the key the curator had given Chet, and returned to tbe geologists' meeting room. No papers were left lying around, and the wastebasket was clean.

Frank went to the blackboard. It had been erased, but a few faint lines were still visible. He studied the chalk markings, which seemed to be part of a map.

"Look over here," he said, stooping down.

In the lower corner of the blackboard, they could make out the words, "low clay."

"What do you imagine that means?" Joe asked.

"Your guess is as good as mine. Maybe if we ask Simmons, he'll have an idea."

The boys left the meeting room and climbed the stairs to the museum's main floor. Rounding a corner into the front hall, they spotted a cluster of policemen.

"I wonder what's up," Frank murmured.

Seeing the young detectives approaching, the police turned to face them.

56

"That's them!" Boswell shouted, stepping out from amongst the cluster of officers and leveling his finger at the trio.

In an instant, the policemen surrounded the boys. "You're under arrest!" one of the officers thundered.

6 A Fortune in Bad Luck

Frank, Joe, and Chet were stunned by the words of the policeman, who stood before them. He flipped his badge at the trio, identifying himself as Detective Barnes from the local precinct.

"Under arrest for what?" Joe blurted.

"We have reason to believe you stole a valuable gem from the museum last night," the detective told Chet, then turned his piercing hazel eyes toward the Hardys. "And we have reason to believe you two conspired in the theft!"

"Why would we want to steal any—" Frank began, but was cut off by the angry curator.

"I don't know who you kids are, but you sure

tried to pull a fast one on me with that phony story," Boswell said acidly.

"We don't have any idea what you're talking about!" Joe cried in defense. "I'm Joe Hardy. He's my brother Frank, and this is Chet Morton, just as we told you yesterday! And we didn't steal any gem!"

"Hold on, Joe," Frank said calmly. He then addressed Detective Barnes in an even tone. "Please explain what this is all about."

"The Faith diamond, which is worth a small fortune, was stolen from its display case sometime during the night," Barnes began. "Curator Boswell tells me you three were caught breaking into the museum yesterday morning. After convincing him that you were involved in an investigation of some kind, you were given a key to the basement entrance and permission to spend the night here."

"I was on a stakeout," Chet agreed.

The police detective continued. "Late in the evening, Chet Morton was caught acting suspiciously in the museum. He was taken to the police station and subsequently released. This morning, the diamond was missing."

"And to think I was fool enough to tell them the security system had been disconnected," Boswell growled. "As far as I know, you three faked the whole thing, names and all. Now let's see some identifications."

The boys pulled out their driver's licenses and handed them to Barnes.

"So that's what that guy was up to last night," Joe whispered to his brother.

"Sure seems like it," Frank agreed.

While the police looked at their licenses, Frank told Detective Barnes about Chet's encounter with the mysterious night visitor.

"I still have to take you to the station," Barnes informed them. "Those licenses could be stolen, and you're the only suspects we have at this point. Also, I'd like you to fill me in on this investigation you claim to be on, as well as on the man you say broke in here last night."

Before leaving the museum, the boys were searched by one of the uniformed policemen, then were led to a waiting squad car. Several reporters tried to question them as they climbed in, but they made no comment.

At the precinct station, Detective Barnes questioned Frank, Joe, and Chet at length about the reasons for their visit to Washington. He then called the Hardy home in Bayport to confirm the story.

Aunt Gertrude answered the phone, and not only corroborated the boys' testimony, but indignantly accused the detective of slandering her nephews.

She had Barnes on the line for five minutes, letting him know Frank and Joe were fine boys, good students, upstanding citizens, and had probably solved more cases than he had in his whole career. The boys could hear the excited voice of their aunt and had difficulty suppressing grins.

Finally, with a groan of relief, the police detective handed the receiver to Frank. "Your aunt wants to talk to you."

"Thanks for the character reference, Aunty," Frank said as he took the phone.

"Don't 'Aunty' me!" came Gertrude Hardy's no-nonsense voice. "What do you mean by smearing our good name up and down the East Coast?"

"What did you say?" Frank raised his voice in alarm.

"I just heard it on the news!" Aunt Gertrude went on. "Sons of well-known detective, Fenton Hardy, suspected of stealing Faith diamond from Smithsonian. I nearly fell off my chair!"

Frank assured his aunt that the matter was being cleared up and that they should be free from all suspicion soon.

"I suggest you see that you are," Aunt Gertrude said abruptly. "And please try to be more careful from now on."

Once Aunt Gertrude was off the line, Detective Barnes offered to release the boys, provided they would not leave the city without notifying him. "You understand you are still under suspicion," he added.

The Hardys promised to keep in touch, and the detective took them back to the museum, where they had left Fritz's car.

"I've always been a big fan of your father's," said Barnes as they drove through the city. "And I hear that you two do quite a job following in his footsteps."

Frank and Joe thanked the detective and waited for him to get to the point he seemed to be making.

Barnes continued. "As long as you are still under suspicion, I thought you might be interested in helping me with this case. I could use you, and the sooner we get to the bottom of this, the sooner your names will be cleared."

"We were thinking the same thing," said Joe. "Are there any clues at this point as to who might have done it?"

"Nothing. Chet's description of a man of medium height and build who wore a ski mask is of little help. But there is an interesting story behind the gem that would be worth looking into."

The detective glanced at Frank and Joe to make sure he had aroused their curiosity, then continued. "The Faith diamond is reputed to bring bad luck to its owners. It was recently acquired by the museum through the will of a man named Arthur Rutlidge. He was a wealthy horse breeder who had been having a devastating run of bad luck with his racehorses. He disappeared in a storm while boating, and presumably drowned."

"Do you think the diamond brought him all that bad luck?" Chet asked.

The detective grinned. "I doubt it. But he willed the stone to the Smithsonian just prior to his disappearance. That's the part I find curious."

"Did Rutlidge know Curator Boswell?" Frank queried.

"I believe they knew each other well," the policeman answered. "Why do you ask?"

"I'm not sure," Frank said thoughtfully. "It's odd Rutlidge would leave the gem to the Smithsonian so shortly before his death, as you said."

Detective Barnes dropped the young sleuths off at the museum, where Fritz's car was still parked.

"Hey, we never had a chance to ask Simmons what those words 'low clay' meant!" Joe said, snapping his fingers.

"We'd better leave that one alone for now," Frank answered. "I doubt either Boswell or Simmons will be very cooperative with us until we clear up the question of the stolen diamond."

The boys were quiet for a moment, then Frank said, "I wonder if Mr. Boswell knows more about this than he lets on. He seemed particularly anxious about the theft, and he was a good friend of Arthur Rutlidge's. Something might add up."

Chet raised his eyebrows at Frank's suggestion. "Are you thinking that Boswell might have taken the stone himself?"

"I know the idea is farfetched," the dark-haired sleuth admitted. "But whoever entered the museum had to have a key to the back door. And it seems odd that the man had a ski mask on, as if he was worried that someone might recognize him."

"I see your point," Joe said. "But the idea is so far out I can't believe it. Anyway, what do we do now?"

"I'll think about it," Frank answered as he squeezed into the driver's seat of Fritz Kriegler's tiny car.

Upon returning to the German Embassy, the three sleuths were met by another gathering.

A group of radio and newspaper reporters waited outside the gate and crowded around them as soon as they arrived. Frank made a short statement for the journalists, saying that the Hardys were in no way connected with the diamond theft, and had been released by the police.

Just then, one of the reporters reached through the open car window and shoved a note into Joe's shirt pocket. Without saying a word, he turned and crossed the street.

Once the newspapermen had left, Joe pulled the note from his pocket and read it aloud: "'PIER SIX AFTER DARK BE THERE WITH DIAMOND. WILL PAY $.'"

"Someone must think we really took that stone," Chet observed.

Frank looked back across the street for the man who had delivered the message, but he was gone. "That's right," he said. "Someone who wants it badly enough to pay for stolen goods."

"Pier six must refer to the city dock," Joe remarked.

"Who cares where it is," Chet spoke up. "We don't have the diamond anyway."

Frank operated the switch on the dashboard to open the embassy gates. "Diamond or not," he said, "this is our chance to find out who wants it and why."

Joe frowned. "I think perhaps we're being set up."

"So do I," Frank concurred. "I'd want Chet and Fritz to be there for cover."

"You plan to walk right into this trap, and I'm supposed to rescue you, is that it?" Chet asked with a tone of disbelief.

"Think of us as live bait," Joe answered. "We'll attract the fish and you can reel him in."

"At least you can help turn the odds in our favor if we do meet with trouble," Frank added.

Once inside the embassy, Frank and Joe described their plan to Fritz. He and Chet were to dress in disguises and be at pier six of the city dock by nightfall. The German youth eagerly agreed to participate in the plan, and he went upstairs to look for material for a disguise.

Frank looked at his watch. "We have a few hours left before dark. Ought to be plenty of time for a little ghost hunting."

7 Unwilling Jockeys

Joe looked at his brother questioningly. "Ghost hunting?"

Frank smiled. "Not real ghosts, but the questions people leave behind about themselves after they're dead. Arthur Rutlidge willed that diamond to the museum very shortly before his boating accident. It's possible that someone associated with him knew he would have that accident."

"You're saying that the drowning may have been on purpose," Joe stated, picking up his brother's thought.

"It's possible. Anyway, Detective Barnes told me that Rutlidge had a horse-breeding farm outside of town. It might be a good idea to check the place out. I'll call the police and tell them we're going. They'll tell whoever is at the manor to let us talk to them."

Less than an hour later, Frank and Joe were driving through thoroughbred racehorse country. Rolling hills covered with dark green grass provided plenty of room for the fast animals to run.

"That must be it," Joe said, indicating an old manor house and several stables set off the road on top of a hill.

Frank turned the red sports car up the long drive. Arriving at the manor house, the boys were met by an old butler who escorted them inside.

The butler introduced himself as Wilkinson as they sat in the living room. "May I bring you some tea?"

The Hardys declined the offer and explained that they were interested in the events surrounding Rutlidge's boating accident.

Wilkinson shook his head. "I was employed by Mr. Rutlidge for close to forty years. He was a grand man, a gentleman and one of the finest breeders in the country. Then a few months ago, everything began to fall to pieces for him."

"How do you mean?" Joe asked.

The butler made a sweeping gesture with his arms. "I mean everything. His best horses could no longer run. Nobody would buy the horses because it was believed the animals were hexed. And then one day, he went sailing on the bay and never came back."

"Why were his horses supposed to be hexed?" Joe questioned the old butler.

"It was that cursed diamond of his. I knew it would get him some day, but he wouldn't let go of it, even when it started to ruin him."

Wilkinson pulled a silk handkerchief from his jacket pocket and gently dabbed his forehead. "I tried persuading him to sell it. I believe several offers were made, although I'm not sure what the conditions were. Anyway, Mr. Rutlidge refused them. He just laughed at the idea that the diamond had any special powers, and seemed almost determined to disprove the superstition. You can see where that got him."

"Who offered to buy the Faith diamond from Rutlidge?" Frank queried.

Wilkinson shrugged. "I don't know. Whoever it was never came here in person." The butler looked quizzically at the boys. "Why are you asking these questions?"

Joe explained that the valuable gem had been stolen from the museum the night before, and that they suspected the theft might be connected with Rutlidge's accident.

"Are you suggesting that this is all part of a plot?" the butler said, raising one eyebrow.

"Could be," Frank answered tersely.

"Is that Mr. Rutlidge?" Joe asked, pointing through the open door to a photograph hanging in the hallway of the old manor house.

A number of pictures covered the walls, mostly of winning thoroughbreds the former horse breeder had raised and owned. In the photograph Joe indicated, a middle-aged man with graying temples stood proudly beside a black filly.

"It was the last picture taken of him," Wilkinson told them. "As a matter of fact, that filly he's with is called Faith. Mr. Rutlidge named her after the diamond. She's a very fast horse now, and she'll be entering her first major race this week."

"This was Rutlidge's way of proving that the Faith diamond didn't have supernatural powers?" Frank asked.

"Exactly." The old butler nodded. "He hoped to clear away the superstition once and for all by actually naming a winning horse after the diamond. Unfortunately, the gem got him first."

"Do you really believe that the diamond has the power to bring bad luck to its owners?" asked Joe, not yet sure whether Wilkinson wasn't exaggerating the story for their benefit.

"All I know," Wilkinson said, as he leaned forward and folded his hands, "is that Mr. Rutlidge isn't the first owner to have met with an untimely end. The last proprietor was lost in an avalanche while skiing in Chile, and the one before him was the victim of a rare tropical disease. Then Mr. Rutlidge, rest his soul, took his sunfish sailboat out for the afternoon and never came back. The next day, the Coast Guard found it washed up on shore all broken up. They concluded that he was caught in a thunderstorm, was thrown off the boat, and drowned. I say he was just another victim of that gem. I hate to admit it, but there's just too much evidence pointing to that stone for me not to believe it has evil powers."

"What about his will?" Frank asked. "He left the diamond to the Smithsonian shortly before his accident. Do you know why?"

"No, I don't. But I do know that his sister, Meg, was quite upset when he made the alteration in the will. They were very close, so when Mr. Rutlidge did this without so much as an explanation, she was surprised and disturbed."

"Does the name Boswell mean anything to you?" Frank asked, changing his line of questioning. "He's the curator of the Smithsonian Museum of Natural History."

Wilkinson brightened. "Oh my, yes! Mr. Rutlidge and Mr. Boswell were childhood friends, and the two saw each other quite often." The butler's smile dropped from his face. "In fact, Mr. Boswell was here for a visit just a couple of days before the terrible accident. Why do you ask?"

"No particular reason," Frank said offhandedly. "Just trying to be thorough. By the way, did Boswell know Meg Rutlidge well, too?"

"Of course," Wilkinson replied. "She's known him all her life."

"How can we get in touch with her?" Frank asked.

"She lives in Baltimore. But you should ask the head trainer, Max, for her exact address. Right now they're trying to settle the estate. Both Meg and Max are supposed to get part, and they're negotiating for it at present."

Frank and Joe thanked Wilkinson for his help. Then they left the old manor house, walking down the hill behind the building to the stables where they found Max. He was shorter than both brothers, and had coarse black hair that seemed to be uncontrollable. His hands were too big for his body.

"Yes, I know the diamond was stolen," Max said after he heard their story. "It was on the radio this morning. Say, aren't you the guys who are supposed to have taken it?"

Frank explained that they hadn't stolen the gem,

and were presently trying to track down the thief who had.

"Well, what brings you out here?" Max asked as he led a horse from its stall and saddled it up. "Mr. Rutlidge gave the diamond to the Smithsonian, and everyone around here is happy to be rid of it. Nothing but bad luck, that stone."

"We find the circumstances of Mr. Rutlidge's streak of bad luck somewhat curious," Frank said. "Especially since he willed the gem just prior to his accident. It was almost as if he knew what might happen, and was trying to prevent someone from getting his hands on it."

Max shot a sharp glance at the young detectives, then grinned. "Why don't we get you a couple of horses and talk about it while we take a ride?"

"Sure, why not?" the boy replied.

The trainer saddled two mares for Frank and Joe. They started out in a trot over the rolling hillside, then slowed to a walk.

"These used to be fine racehorses," Max said as he pulled alongside Frank and Joe. "Trained them myself. Too old to race anymore, though. We just use them for breeding."

Upon further questioning, the boys learned that Rutlidge's sister had wanted the Faith diamond very much, and had prepared a case to get it back legally from the Smithsonian. Max gave them her address in Baltimore.

Suddenly the sleuths' horses took off as if out of the starting gate of a racetrack. The jolt nearly knocked the boys out of their saddles. Frank managed to grab his reins when his thoroughbred spooked, but Joe had dropped his, and now he hugged the animal's neck as it sped at a full gallop across the field.

However, he gradually began to lose his grip. He tried in vain to slow the animal, which seemed to be driven by some invisible force. Finally, Joe's arm slid from the horse's neck. He grabbed a piece of the saddle, but his balance was going.

"Hold on, Joe!" Frank yelled. He had gained some control over his horse and was pulling alongside his brother. "Jump!" he shouted, urging Joe to leap from one speeding animal to the other.

"I can't!" the younger Hardy yelled back. His foot had become twisted in his stirrup. If he fell now, he would be dragged along under the frenzied racehorse! Yet he knew he wouldn't be able to hold the saddle much longer.

Then, just as suddenly, both horses slowed down and came to a stop. The wild impulse that had possessed them left them the same instant.

"These old beauties still have plenty of steam left in them," Joe groaned as he disentangled himself

from the stirrup and climbed down. "I wonder what caused them to spook like that."

Max rode up to the Hardys. "Are you okay?" he asked worriedly.

"We're alive," Frank answered with a frown.

"I'm sorry," Max went on. "Sometimes these thoroughbreds get the idea they're back at the racetrack, and they just take off, each trying to outrun the other."

"You could've warned us," Joe grumbled.

Max shrugged and turned back toward the stables.

"Do you think he knew these horses would spook?" Joe murmured to his brother.

"It might have been a good way to put an end to our questions," Frank replied, watching Max disappear up the hill.

"Let's ask *him* a few questions, like where he was last night when the diamond was stolen," Joe said hotly.

Frank shrugged. "I don't think he'd cooperate. Meg Rutlidge might be a better bet at this point. Boswell didn't tell Detective Barnes that she had been trying to reclaim the stone. If he was trying to cover for someone by accusing Chet of the theft, it may have been Meg!"

"But Chet saw a man enter the museum," Joe argued.

"That doesn't mean she didn't have something to do with it."

The two sleuths took their horses back to the estate. Max had gone, and one of the stable hands led the animals to their stalls.

"We'd better return to town," Joe said as they walked to the car. "We have an appointment at the city dock."

It was dark by the time the two arrived in Washington. The dock was located along the Potomac River in the heart of the city. When he found the pier marked number six, Frank pulled the red sports car over to the curb and stopped.

"Well, here we are," he murmured. "I just hope Chet and Fritz are around. This could be trouble."

8 A Clever Deal

Pier six was empty except for two people fishing from the end of the dock. They wore wide-brimmed hats and brightly colored shirts. Figuring them to be Fritz and Chet, the Hardys chuckled at the corny disguise and strolled out on the pier to let them know they had arrived.

"Pssst," Frank whispered loudly as they drew near, "seen anyone around?"

"Nobody but you guys!" a rough voice answered as the two fishermen jumped to their feet and lunged at Frank and Joe!

Caught off guard, the boys found themselves in the clutches of two strange thugs before they could react.

"We'll take that stone now," Frank's captor demanded. He was a big man with a low, gravelly voice.

"What about the money?" Frank challenged, playing along.

"We'll let you have the money when we see the stone," the man replied, tightening his wrestling hold on Frank.

"That sounds fair." The older Hardy pretended to give in. "But I left it in the car. I'll go and get it for you."

"Go ahead. But if you try anything stupid, remember your brother is with us," the hefty man snarled.

He released Frank, who took one step down the pier, then whirled around and caught him with his fist just above the jaw. In the same instant, Joe hooked his foot around his captor's leg and brought him to the ground.

Fists flew for a few rounds between the battling pairs at the end of the pier, but Frank and Joe were in better physical shape and soon gained the upper hand over their tiring assailants.

Just then, one of the men hesitated for a second and gestured to his companion to retreat. Both took off down the pier with Joe in pursuit. Frank, however, stood still and stared out across the dark water. He had seen one of the men glance beyond

79

him just before they broke off the fight, as if looking for a signal from somewhere out in the anchorage that lay beyond the docks.

"What happened to you?" Joe said accusingly to his dark-haired brother as he returned from his chase. "I couldn't handle both of those guys all by myself."

"I think I know who arranged this little surprise party," Frank answered. "See that ship anchored over there?"

Joe peered out on the water. A sixty-foot motor yacht lay in the bay, gleaming in the moonlight.

"Someone was on deck watching the whole show through binoculars," Frank went on. "When I spotted him, he put down the glasses and ducked beneath the railing."

The Hardys hurried to a small marina nearby, where the lights were on. They knocked on the door, and a portly, red-faced dock master greeted them.

"Did you see a couple of guys on the pier with fishing poles and wide hats?" Joe queried.

The dock master let out a big belly laugh. "You'd be lucky to catch a boot in these waters. Nobody with any sense would go fishing around here. Now if you're looking for crabs, that's a different story."

"So you haven't seen two men with fishing poles," Frank interrupted.

The portly dock master shook his head.

"What about the yacht anchored out in the basin?" Joe asked. "Do you know anything about it?"

"Sure do. A fellow named Jensen owns that beauty. Wayne Jensen is his name. He's been moored out there for a couple of months." The dock master paused. "Say, you youngsters look like you've been in a fight or something."

"We were mugged," Frank said tersely, "And we think Mr. Jensen could have had a hand in it."

"I hardly think Mr. Jensen has to mug people to make money," the portly man told them, his deep laugh bubbling up again. "But if you'd like to discuss it with him, I'll let you use a dinghy to row out there."

The brothers thanked the dock master, who led them to one of several dinghies he had tied at the dock. Just as Frank and Joe were getting in, though, two figures appeared in the darkness equipped with fishing poles and wide hats.

"Are those the fellows you were talking about?" the dock master asked.

Without answering, Frank and Joe ran to intercept the muggers. The two tried to avoid them but Frank and Joe stopped them in their tracks with flying tackles. The four landed together in a heap on the ground.

"Hey, what are you guys trying to prove?" a youthful voice cried out.

The Hardys immediately realized that they had just tackled Chet and Fritz! The four got to their feet and dusted themselves off as Frank and Joe apologized and explained their mistake.

"What took you so long to get here, anyway?" Frank questioned his friends. "We could've used your help a few minutes ago."

Fritz explained that he and Chet had come on a couple of motorcycles he kept in his garage. When they left the embassy, the same gray Peugeot that had followed him to the airport had pulled out behind them. He and Chet then took different routes, finally shaking the sedan.

Chet drew a rolled up newspaper from his back pocket. "The evening paper just came out. It mentions our names in connection with the diamond theft."

Joe opened up the paper to a small article on the theft. It said that the trio had been released, but were still under suspicion.

"Come on," Frank told his blond brother, "with a little luck, we might be able to clear this thing up tonight."

Leaving Chet and Fritz at the dock to stand guard, Frank and Joe climbed into the dinghy and rowed out to Wayne Jensen's boat.

The night was clear, and the light from a full moon glittered off the surface of the calm Potomac River. As the sleuths drew near the large motor yacht, they could see a man on the aft deck watching their approach. The boat was even more luxurious than they had guessed from a distance. It looked to be capable of long ocean voyages.

The man aboard the yacht stood up and dropped a ladder over its side.

"Howdy, boys. What can I do for you? I'm Wayne Jensen," he said with a Texas accent as they pulled the dinghy alongside the sixty-foot vessel.

"He's not the phony reporter who put the note in my pocket," Joe said. "But no doubt he's the one who hired that guy."

After obtaining permission to climb aboard, Frank explained that he had some merchandise the man might be interested in.

Jensen eyed the two youths suspiciously. "What are you talking about?"

"Look," said Frank, "we saw you with your binoculars, watching us as we were jumped on the pier. So don't play innocent."

"Yes, I saw the fight," Jensen admitted, "and I got my binoculars to see what was going on. I would have called the police, but you seemed to be handling the situation very well by yourselves. Probably a couple of muggers, right?"

"No. We had a date with those guys. They were going to buy something from us," Frank said slowly.

"Oh?"

"And we're ready to sell it to you if you have the money!"

Jensen's smile left his face. "I still have no idea what you are driving at, but whatever it is you're involved in, you're barking up the wrong tree."

Frank put his hand in his pocket. He was clearly carrying a small, round object, which he played with in his pocket. Jensen stared at it for a second and a look of anxiety crossed his face.

"What are you boys trying to peddle on me, anyway?" he asked.

"Just a stone," Frank answered.

"What kind of stone?"

Joe handed the Texan the newspaper and pointed out the article on the stolen diamond. The man quickly read it.

"Are you telling me you have this gem with you?" Jensen said coldly. "I could see to it that you're arrested."

"We're not saying anything," Frank answered. "But if you want to buy what I have, this is your last chance to make an offer."

Wayne Jensen sat still, glaring at his visitors.

"Okay," he said at last, "I'll give you fifty thousand for it."

"The stone's all yours," Frank said evenly as he pulled a large pebble from his pocket and flipped it at the wealthy yachtsman.

9 The Racer's Edge

Anger flashed across the Texan's face. "Just what are you trying to prove with this stupid charade?" he snapped, hurling the worthless pebble overboard.

"We want to know why a man like you is so anxious to get hold of the Faith diamond, even as stolen property," Joe told him. "If you don't mind answering a few questions, we won't tell the police that you had us attacked and offered to buy the gem."

"You can't prove anything," Jensen replied hotly. "Now get off of this boat before I have to throw you off!"

"Certainly," Frank said. "It was a pleasure meeting you."

The boys climbed down the ladder into their dinghy, feeling like sitting ducks. They did not breathe easy until they had reached the pier and joined their friends.

"What happened out there?" Chet asked as he grabbed the painter from Joe and fastened it to a piling.

"Frank's quite a salesman," Joe said proudly. "He almost sold a piece of gravel for fifty thousand bucks."

"I just wanted Jensen to admit he was after the gem," the older Hardy said. "Now we have to figure out why."

Fritz gazed at the motor yacht gleaming in the pale moonlight. "It looks like your friend is making his getaway!"

They could hear the sound of the yacht's engines starting up, and two men were on the bow pulling up the anchor. In less than a minute, the sixty-foot cruiser was on its way out of the basin and into the Potomac River.

Upon returning to the dock house, Frank and Joe questioned the dock master as to where Jensen might be headed. The jolly man could tell them only that the yacht sometimes left for one or two days. He wasn't sure where it went, but it couldn't go far in that time.

"Has Jensen bought any charts lately?" Frank asked.

"I seem to recall that he has," the dock master answered, scratching his head. "I believe he bought several of the Potomac River and Chesapeake Bay area. He also got one of Baltimore Harbor."

Thanking the dock master for his help, the four youths returned to the embassy. They kept an eye out for the gray sedan that had followed Chet and Fritz earlier, but it was not in sight.

"Do you think the Rabbit was driving that Peugeot?" Chet asked once they were in the German Embassy.

"Either he was or someone else who's very interested in us," Frank replied. "I hope the ambassador heard from Dad today. I'm getting edgy about this whole business."

But Ambassador Kriegler still had not received any word from Fenton Hardy. Frank and Joe had a fitful night's sleep.

In the morning, Frank called Detective Barnes for further information on the diamond theft. The police detective told them that he would run a check on Wayne Jensen, and that as yet he had no substantial leads on the missing gem.

Then Frank contacted Sam Radley in Bayport,

who reported that Dr. Hasso Werner was a very well-known geologist who taught at a German university. He was a good family man, and his record was clean.

"Maybe Dr. Werner's team is on the level after all," Joe commented. "It could have been just plain coincidence that they were meeting in the museum on Tuesday."

Frank shook his head. "Too many coincidences are adding up. Werner has the initials H. W., he's German, and he was there that morning. On top of that, there's something too secretive about him and his party."

"And we still don't know where he is." Joe shrugged, seeing his brother's point. "We ought to pursue that clue we found on their blackboard. 'Low clay' just might lead us to the geologist. If Dad is in trouble, we shouldn't be wasting our time chasing the diamond."

"Unless the theft ties in with Dad's case," Frank pointed out. "It's also quite a coincidence the Faith diamond was stolen the same day we got here."

The blond sleuth nodded. "I just wish Dad would call to fill us in on some of this stuff and tell us he's okay. I'm also shaky about the Rabbit. We haven't had a bomb thrown at us for two days, and it makes me wonder whether he isn't cooking up something really nasty."

"It's possible," Frank said, trying to play down the thought. "But I have a feeling that the Rabbit's job is over. Even if he didn't blow us to bits, he diverted us from the case long enough for us to lose the scent."

"Let's sure hope so!" Chet piped in. "One more sign of that guy and I'm back in Bayport!"

Over breakfast, the amateur detectives decided to pay a visit to Meg Rutlidge in Baltimore. They borrowed Fritz's two motorcycles since he was using the car. The bikes were German-made, light and swift. In less than an hour the boys were in Baltimore, a major port for commerce on the Eastern Seaboard.

Meg Rutlidge lived in a townhouse in the center of the city. She was hesitant to talk to Frank and Joe, but at last convinced of their sincerity, she opened up.

"Yes, I've been trying to reclaim Arthur's diamond from the Smithsonian," the kindly, refined woman said. "My brother had always promised me I would have it someday. Then his racehorses began performing poorly and that old superstition about the stone's power to bring bad luck came up."

"So Mr. Rutlidge changed his will, giving the diamond to the museum and protecting you from its so-called curse?" Frank guessed.

Meg nodded. "He told me when he changed the

will that he was doing it for my own good. He said he was convinced the gem had some kind of evil power. The funny thing is, until that day he had always laughed at the superstition. He even had a young racehorse named after the diamond, just so he could dispel the myth."

"Your brother's butler told us about the horse," Joe said. "She's supposed to run her first major race in a couple of days."

"Yes, but Arthur won't be there," Meg said sadly. She sat silently in thought for a moment, then went on. "In any case, I thought it was very strange that he had that change of heart over the diamond. He knew the gem had about as much supernatural powers as the kitchen sink. He couldn't have been in his right mind when he made out that new will."

"And that's why you made your case to reclaim the Faith diamond from the museum," Frank deduced.

"Yes," the woman answered softly. "Only now there's no diamond to reclaim. I hope you boys find the thief who took it."

"Did a man named Jensen ever offer to buy it?" Frank queried.

"Not that I know of," Meg Rutlidge said. "If an offer was made, Arthur didn't mention it to me."

"What about the museum curator, Mr. Boswell?" the older Hardy asked casually, but watched for her response to the name. "I hear that you and Arthur were both good friends of his."

"Arthur was and I still am," Meg replied, giving no sign of being jarred by the question. "Why do you want to know?"

The sleuths explained that they had a hunch the curator might know more about the diamond's theft than he let on. The fact that Arthur Rutlidge's accident left some peculiar questions of its own, and that he was a friend of Boswell's, might tie in with the case.

Meg stared out the window, distracted by a thought. "David Boswell phoned me this morning," she said at last. "It was just a social call. He apologized for the loss of the diamond, knowing how much I had wanted it back. We talked about it for a while. But I couldn't help thinking that there was something else he meant to tell me and didn't."

"Does he believe in the stone's curse?" Joe asked.

"No. He's even helped me in my case to reclaim the diamond," Meg said, leaning back in her chair with a sigh. "He was planning to testify on my behalf that Arthur must have been out of his mind when he changed the will."

Convinced that Rutlidge's sister knew nothing about the gem's disappearance, Frank and Joe thanked her and left. They mounted their motorcycles and drove down to the harbor to see if Jensen's ship was there. The harbor was busy with traffic, but the large yacht wasn't among it.

The sleuths then made a stop at a special museum of horse racing, a small brick building near the harbor. A collection of films was available to the public for viewing, and the brothers picked out one in which Rutlidge's entry had lost unexpectedly. In a small viewing room, they threaded the spool into a projector and turned out the lights.

By stopping the film, running it in reverse, and then forward again in slow motion, Frank and Joe could see that Rutlidge's horse seemed to break stride during the race just as it rounded the far turn.

"Look at the way its ears perk up just before it loses its pace," Joe said. He stopped the projector, freezing the animal's motion as it rounded the turn.

"It sure appears as if the horse sensed something that made it falter," Frank agreed. "Almost as if it was trained to react to a signal."

"You think someone conditioned it to lose?" Joe asked, finding his brother's idea hard to swallow.

"Let's just say it might be time to ask Rutlidge's trainer, Max, a few questions."

The boys returned the film, left the museum, and rode over the hilly country roads that led to the Rutlidge estate.

They were not far from the city, however, when Joe's bike developed engine trouble. He had to coast down a hill and pull into a service station.

"I'm a biker myself," the attendant told the Hardys as he stepped away from the gas pumps to inspect Joe's motorcycle. "Haven't seen any like these around here, though. I bet I can fix 'em anyway."

The lanky young man wheeled Joe's bike into the garage and brought out a set of tools he used on his own machine. "Are you guys on the way to the cliffs?" he asked.

"What cliffs?" Frank inquired.

"I take my bike there all the time," the young man said as he pointed with a wrench to a motor- cycle in the corner of the garage. "Best biking in the area.

Frank glanced at the bike. It was covered with yellowish mud. "Looks like you drive it hard," he observed. "That mud's pretty thick."

"It's not mud," the youth answered. "It's clay, yellow clay. You get that down at the cliffs."

Frank and Joe instantly had the same thought. Could the words "low clay" they had found on the geologist's blackboard have been what was left of "yellow clay?"

"These cliffs are made of yellow clay?" Frank asked to get the story straight.

The lanky gas station attendant looked up from his work. "They're called the Yellow Clay Cliffs."

"You didn't see a group of scientists down there recently, did you?" Joe asked. "They would be drilling the ground?"

"So that's what those guys were up to," the youth said, his interest showing. "Geologists, huh? I saw them working at the base of the cliffs just this morning!"

10 Follow the Yellow Clay Road

Frank and Joe decided to put off returning to the Rutlidge estate. While Joe helped to fix his motorcycle, the older Hardy made a phone call to Washington. Since the boys were still officially suspects in the diamond burglary, they had to make regular contact with the police to inform them of their whereabouts.

Barnes had dug up some material on Wayne Jensen and related his findings over the phone. Jensen had indeed made a fortune. But a great part of his earnings were either undocumented or suspect, and were centered around dealings with foreign concerns.

"Let's go," Joe called out as his brother returned from making the call. "My bike's humming like new."

He took a few laps around the pumps to make sure the engine was working properly, then waved to the station attendant and wheeled back on the road. Frank took off after him.

In time, the steep hills gave way to much lower and flatter terrain covered with thick underbrush. Following the gas station attendant's directions, the two sleuths took a road that led down to the shores of the lower Potomac, where the river emptied into the wide Chesapeake Bay.

The road followed the river for a short while before the terrain began rising again. In moments, the boys found themselves on a narrow lane, cut high into the wall of the bluffs that towered above the water. The bluffs were jagged from erosion, and the road wound around them in sharp curves.

It continued rising until it reached the top of the bluffs, more than a hundred feet over the river and bay. There, dense pine forest covered the land. Except for a few dirt lanes running into the woods, there were no signs of civilization in the area.

Taking it slowly along the dangerous terrain, the Hardys kept an eye out for the geologists. At one spot, the cliffs suddenly became a deep yellow hue.

Now the brothers traveled over a hard clay surface, making traction considerably worse for the motorcycle tires.

"That guy at the gas station has got to be some kind of daredevil to take his bike out here for kicks," Joe shouted above the noise of the engines.

"When this stuff gets wet, it must be especially treacherous," Frank called back.

Following the dangerous road for another mile, the sleuths came to a point where the yellow clay ended. Beyond it, the ground once again became dirt brown.

"We must have missed them," Joe said, swinging his motorcycle around. "Let's take it slower this time."

The boys drove back and forth over the area of the bluffs marked by the yellowish clay, but they saw no sign of the geologists whom the gas station attendant had told them about.

Joe braked his bike and waited for his brother to catch up. The day was growing hot, and he used a rag from his back pocket to wipe his neck and forehead, grimy with a combination of dirt and sweat.

"Do you think they've already packed up and left?" Frank asked as he pulled alongside Joe's motorcycle.

"I don't know," Joe responded. "Maybe we

should try exploring some of those dirt paths leading back in the woods."

They started their bikes up again, heading toward the top of the bluffs.

Just then, a pickup truck came from around a corner in the road. Both boys swerved hard to avoid the oncoming vehicle.

"That's the geologists' truck," Joe yelled. The Hardys spun their bikes in a one-hundred-and-eighty-degree turn and started down the road after it.

Following at a distance, they trailed the pickup back to an area where the road widened. The truck parked on the shoulder. A man got out and climbed down a small trench cut diagonally in the steep bluff.

Waiting until he was out of sight, the brothers drove up to the truck and peered toward the water. On the beach at the foot of the bluff were the geologists! The equipment they used for boring core samples was in operation. It was an elaborate rig and most of the men were working on it. A makeshift dock had been built nearby.

"Werner must be among them," Joe said excitedly as he started down the crude path.

"Wait a minute," said Frank, grabbing his brother's arm. "If we barge in like that, we might blow our chances of finding out what they're up to."

"You're right," Joe agreed, and climbed back to

the road. "Those men may not be as harmless as they seem."

Staying out of sight, the young detectives mounted their motorcycles and headed down the yellow clay road. They found a small fishing village further along the shoreline, a couple of miles from where the cliffs began.

"Can we rent a skiff with an outboard somewhere in town?" Frank asked a group of men who sat in rocking chairs on the front porch of the village's general store.

"You boys want to go fishing?" one of the men asked, bringing his rocker to a stop.

"In a way, we do," Frank responded.

The man stood up from his rocker. "Come on along then. I've got something you can use. It's ten dollars a day, not including the cost of gas."

The brothers agreed to the fisherman's terms.

Joe went to inspect the skiff to be sure the engine worked, and to check for leaks. Frank, meanwhile, called Chet and Fritz from the general store and asked them to meet the Hardys in the village as soon as possible. He also suggested that they bring along the disguises they had used the previous evening, and get two more for Frank and Joe. They would also need a tent, sleeping bags, and camping supplies.

100

An hour later, Fritz's sports car pulled up in front of the general store.

"We have everything you guys asked for," Chet announced. "What's the plan?"

Frank told him that, disguised as a group of boys out on a fishing trip, they would "accidentally stumble" on Werner's team. They could set up camp on the beach near the geologists, pretending to be just a bunch of curious youngsters.

"So the idea is to play dumb," Joe put in. "That should be easy for some of us."

Still embarrassed over the episode in the dark museum, Chet ignored Joe's kidding. "Just wait. You'll be glad I came along."

Donning sunglasses, hats, and fishing poles, the foursome manned the skiff and headed down the shoreline. As they rounded a turn under the bluffs, Joe slowed the boat. The others threw out lines, as if trolling for fish. The geologists looked up from their work when they saw the young people approach, and Joe turned their boat toward the beach.

"Howdy!" Frank called out with a big smile. "What's going on?"

The men returned the greeting with rude stares, then resumed their work. Frank, Joe, and Chet got out of the skiff and walked up the beach, joining the workers around the equipment.

101

"Are you drilling for oil or something?" Joe asked with a hokey accent. "Gee whiz, that sure is a weird contraption you've got there."

A slightly balding man of medium build stepped from the machinery. He had dark eyes and a neatly cropped beard. "What do you want?" he asked with a thick German accent.

"Oh, we're just fishing," Frank answered. "Weren't getting any bites, though, so we thought we'd say hi and find out what's going on."

"We're taking core samples," the bearded man replied tersely.

"Then you're scientists?" Frank asked.

"Yes, and we're very busy. So if you will excuse us."

"Hey, this stuff is neat," Chet said as he wandered around the drilling equipment. "What are these things for?" He pointed to a couple of long cylinders lying on the beach.

"Boring rods," the scientist answered. "Don't touch anything."

"Why are you taking core samples around here?" Frank pursued the questioning.

A large, burly man came over to him. "Get out of here. You are bothering us," he ordered.

"Sorry," Frank said, backing off. "We were just curious. We'd be happy to help with the drilling if you are behind schedule or something."

"We don't want your help," the burly man replied gruffly. "We want you to get out of here."

The four boys, seeing that they would be physically evicted from the site unless they left on their own, prepared to go back to the skiff.

"Nice to meet you," Frank said with a smile and extended his hand to the bearded scientist. "By the way, I'm John Sterret. I didn't catch your name."

The man, happy to be rid of the nosy boys, quickly shook hands. "I'm Dr. Werner. Sorry we're too busy to chat."

The sleuths returned to their boat, where Fritz had already started up the motor in case trouble erupted.

"We should've let him know who we were and why we're here," Joe said to his brother.

"Maybe later," Frank decided. "Right now we're not sure if he's friend or foe. The odds would be against us if Frank and Joe Hardy were names that spelled 'enemy' for Werner."

"If you saw what I saw, you'd be glad you gave him that phony name," Chet spoke up. "That man is no friend. One of those cylinders had the infinity sign drawn on it!"

11 Sunset Oystermen

Joe shot an astonished look at his friends, then at the team of geologists on the beach. "You mean, Werner's in cahoots with the Rabbit?"

"Cool it," Frank urged his brother. "Don't pay any more attention to them. Just head this thing down the shore."

The boys threw out fishing lines as Joe motored the skiff around a bend in the high bluffs. Once they were out of sight, they drew in the lines and took off their disguises.

"This seems like a good spot to set up camp," Frank said, indicating an area where the bluffs had eroded enough to provide a naturally protected section of the beach.

The foursome pitched Fritz's tent at the foot of the yellow clay cliff. Frank and Joe collected driftwood, as Chet and Fritz prepared to make supper. By the time the sun began to set over the wide, still waters of the lower Potomac, the boys had a pot of beef stew bubbling over a crackling fire.

"I feel like a gypsy camping on the Rhine River," Fritz remarked wistfully, remembering the natural beauty of his own part of the world. "Now all we need is a violin and a tambourine."

"I feel like an early American explorer," Chet said, and gazed over the water. The far shore was lined with a dense forest that broke off at the point where the Potomac fed into the bay. "Only now we don't have to worry about hostile Indians or wild animals. We can just enjoy the sunset over the river."

Joe, relaxing against a log, chuckled at his chunky friend's observation. "No, we don't have to worry about wild animals, just bomb-throwing terrorists. If given a choice, I'd go for the animals."

The four youths sat in quiet thought as the sun turned a deep red hue and sank into the horizon. A boat loaded with oysters came into sight. Moving slowly with its heavy cargo piled high in the middle, it made an odd silhouette against the sunset. Two men were aboard and, noticing the camp fire on the beach, watched the four boys as they went by.

"They must be from the fishing village," Joe said. "Looks like they made a good harvest today." He stood up and waved at the oystermen, who returned the wave before disappearing around the bend.

"I wish we had some of those fresh oysters to make a stew," Chet put in.

Joe let out a groan. "How can you think about food right now? I'm stuffed."

"Wait a minute," Frank said. "This isn't oyster season. Those couldn't have been fresh oysters."

"Are you suggesting that the boat was full of rotten oysters?" Chet said.

"Look," Frank told him. "Oysters are not in season during the summer. They're only harvested in the months that have an 'r' in their spelling— September through April. I don't know what those guys are up to, but they're sure not oystermen!"

Suddenly, Frank and Joe had the same thought. The boat might not have been on its way to the fishing village at all!

"Let's check on the geologists," Frank said to his younger brother.

Both boys got to their feet and jogged down the beach in the direction of the drilling site. It was dark by the time they arrived. The oyster boat was nosed up on the beach and several men were in the process of unloading something.

Hoping the men were too busy to notice them, the two sleuths crept closer to the drilling site to get a better look. Concealed under the mound of oysters were several core cylinders, which the men unloaded and carefully carried up on the beach.

Frank nudged his brother's arm and pointed to the pickup truck parked on the bluff road. As the geologists finished their business, the boys scaled the steep path up the bluff. They climbed in the back of the truck, covered themselves with the canvas tarp, and waited.

In a few minutes, they could hear two men approaching. One of them was clearly Dr. Werner. The other sounded like the one who had threatened the boys earlier. In listening to the two talk, Frank and Joe learned that his name was Roget. Although he spoke German, he clearly had a French accent.

The two men climbed into the cab of the pickup. A second later, the engine started up and they were on their way down the bluff road.

"This guy drives like a maniac!" Joe exclaimed in a whisper as the truck sped around the sharp bends in the road, tossing its hidden occupants back and forth under the canvas tarp. "Next time I hitch a ride, it'll be with someone who I know can drive."

After some adjustment of their bodies, they found that they could brace themselves between the sides of the truck without getting thrown around too much. Once settled, they discussed their next move.

"The geologists, or whatever they are, were using those oyster shells to cover their cargo of core cylinders," Frank observed. "They wanted it to appear as though they were going out empty in the morning, then returning in the evening laden with a harvest of oysters."

"But they were really going out full at night and coming back empty in the morning," Joe finished Frank's deduction.

"Exactly. Also, there were nine geologists at the Smithsonian for Werner's meeting. Only five were at the drilling site. If the two men in the oyster boat were part of the team, that leaves two remaining men unaccounted for. They might be where the cylinders were coming from."

"Do you think the Rabbit is one of the two missing guys?" Joe asked nervously.

"No. He was busy hassling us while the meeting was being held. But Chet saw the cylinder with the infinity sign on it, so that proves he's associated with this outfit. In any case, I have the impression that Dr. Werner isn't the head honcho in this operation. We ought to stay under cover for the time being until we can determine a little more clearly just what's going on."

The young detectives felt the pickup truck turn off the road and go up a gravel drive. Soon it came to a stop. They waited for the men to leave, then peeked out from under the tarp. They found themselves outside a small bungalow set back in the woods at the top of the yellow clay cliffs. The two cars that they had seen leaving the Smithsonian were also parked in front of the house.

"This must be where the gang's staying," Joe said excitedly.

Frank was puzzled. "If those are the cars that carried the geologists, why aren't they down at the drilling site? It doesn't make sense. How do the men get back here to sleep without their cars?"

"Perhaps they camp at the drilling site," Joe said.

The older boy shook his head. "I didn't see any tents or camping gear there."

"Well, maybe they travel on the oyster boat," Joe suggested. "It seems to me we should follow that boat and see where it comes from."

Frank nodded. "That might be the answer. But let's try a little old-fashioned eavesdropping first."

The sleuths threw off the tarp and hopped from the pickup truck. The sky was overcast, making it darker than it had been on the previous evening. This provided good cover for the boys to sneak up on the house without being noticed.

Lights were on in the bungalow. Dr. Werner and

Roget could be seen through the window engaged in conversation. The Hardys stationed themselves outside and listened. The muffled voices were barely audible. Roget did most of the talking, appearing loud and argumentative.

Frank and Joe crept around the bungalow, hoping to find an open window. But as they did, Werner stood up and went to the door. A ferocious-looking dog jumped to its feet. It was a Doberman pinscher that had been lying in a corner. Werner opened the door, letting the animal out.

The Doberman sensed Frank and Joe almost immediately and emitted a low growl.

"Let's get out of here," Joe cried under his breath.

As soon as the boys dashed away from the house, the vicious dog began barking. It lurched forward in pursuit, and before they knew it, the amateur detectives found themselves cornered at the top of the cliff. The Doberman's bark turned into a bare-teethed snarl when it found its prey trapped. The dog approached slowly and deliberately. Neither boy dared move.

"When I say jump, jump," Frank said, just barely moving his lips. The beach lay far below, but the incline of the bluff face would help break their fall. If they were lucky, they would get away with only minor injuries!

12 A Mysterious Signal

The beast drew closer, exposing canine fangs, until it was no more than a few feet from the frightened youths.

Suddenly, the Doberman's ears perked up. It seemed to linger in a moment of indecision, first looking back at the bungalow, then turning toward Frank and Joe with a snarl. Finally, the animal reluctantly retreated from the cliff and returned to the bungalow.

"What happened?" Joe gasped, amazed by the abrupt shift in their fortune.

"Werner probably called the dog back inside," Frank answered. "And not a second too soon."

"I didn't hear anything," Joe said.

"Remember the werewolf case?" the older Hardy asked, referring to *Night of the Werewolf,* a recent mystery the brothers had solved by tracking down the secret behind a killer beast that glowed in the dark.

"Yes, the crook in that case was using a dog whistle," Joe said, slapping his forehead for not having thought of it himself. "Werner must have used one of those things too!"

"Right," Frank went on. "The pitch of the whistle was too high for us to hear. Only dogs can . . . Wait a second!" Frank's voice rose in excitement. "Max, the horse trainer, had something hanging around his neck that looked like one of those whistles. I hadn't thought of it before, but there's no reason why an ordinary dog whistle couldn't be used on a horse!"

"It might account for the strange way those two horses spooked on us," Joe said, snapping his fingers.

"Not only that," Frank put in. "It might also account for the way Rutlidge's horses lost those races. They may have been trained to respond to a whistle!"

Vowing to return to the Rutlidge estate as soon as possible, the amateur detectives walked back down the bluff road.

But before they had gone more than a few

hundred feet, the geologists' pickup truck swung out of the driveway. Its headlight beams nearly caught Frank and Joe in the road, but the boys dove out of the way and threw themselves face down in a ditch as the truck sped past.

"I wonder if they're going back to the drilling site," said Joe as he stood up and tried to wipe off the sticky yellow clay smeared on his knees and elbows. "Maybe another shipment is coming in."

The two sleuths watched the truck disappear around a curve. A minute later it appeared again in the distance, rounding the next bend in the cliffs. It came to a stop on a promontory, pointing out over the dark expanse of the bay. Then its headlights flashed on and off three times.

"They're signaling," Joe said, as he watched the truck's lights flash again.

For a moment nothing happened. Then from far out on the bay came three answering flashes.

Immediately, Frank drew an arrow in the clay with his finger. It pointed in the exact direction of the answering signal. By reading the stars, he soon determined that the flashes had come from east by northeast.

"I'll bet that's where the oyster boat started out," Joe deduced.

"And possibly where our two missing geologists, if not the Rabbit himself, are located," Frank added.

114

The brothers continued, hoping to find a route down the bluff without having to go all the way back to the drilling site. Luckily, they discovered a shallow groove cut diagonally in the clay all the way to the beach. Taking it slowly, the boys descended along the groove, ending up a short distance from camp.

"Hey, what happened to you guys?" a worried Chet asked, as his bedraggled friends stumbled into camp.

Frank and Joe told their story to Chet and Fritz, then curled up in sleeping bags and fell fast asleep. They didn't wake until the smell of sizzling bacon wafted into their tent in the morning. Putting on a clean set of clothes, the brothers stepped out into the sun.

Chet sat in the sand with an open book in his lap. "I've been reading up on earthquakes," he said, flipping the page. "Did you know that tidal waves are caused by earthquakes in the ocean floor?"

"Yes, Chet," Frank replied. "Did you know that your bacon is burnt to a crisp?"

Chet dropped his book and forked what was left of his breakfast from the pan. With a shrug, he discarded the charred bacon, then put a few fresh strips in. "As I was saying," he went on, as he sat down with his book again, "tidal waves can travel hundreds of miles in a few minutes, and rise as high as a hundred feet or more by the time they hit shore. Can you imagine sitting at the beach when a hundred-foot wave suddenly comes out of nowhere? That's as big as a building!"

"Have you read about any quakes like the one we had in Bayport?" Joe asked.

Chet sniffed. "That one was too small to even count. There are around fifty thousand earthquakes every year."

"If it had damaged that nuclear power plant much more, it would've counted for plenty," said Frank, remembering how frightened Biff's uncle had been that the reactor core might have become cracked.

Conversation among the boys stopped when the oyster boat came into sight around the bluff. It was empty of its phony cargo.

"If we could do it without being spotted, this would be the perfect time to follow those guys," Joe remarked as he pulled his hat brim over his eyes to avoid the possibility of being recognized.

"Except we *would* be spotted," Frank said. "Also, we should pick up an extra can of fuel before we go on any long trips in the bay."

After breakfast, Frank and Joe took the skiff back to the fishing village. Fritz and Chet stayed to mind the camp and keep a lookout for any new developments.

At the village, the brothers found the man who

had rented them the skiff. He supplied them with an extra fuel can, and asked, "Did you catch anything yesterday?"

Frank shook his head. "No. We were thinking about heading farther into the bay, east by northeast. Any good spots out that way?"

"East by northeast? That ought to take you around Chapel Island. Not sure you'll find much fish there, except you might hook a bass if you're lucky."

"What's Chapel Island like?" Frank asked as he filled the fuel tank from a gas pump outside the general store.

The fisherman's face screwed up in a curious expression. "It's a strange island. Some folks moved there close to two hundred years ago, and to this day the same families live there, descendants of the original settlers. They don't mix with mainlanders. Stranger than that, for all appearances they still are living in the eighteenth century. Still speak the Queen's English."

Frank and Joe exchanged glances. Had the signals the night before come from Chapel Island?

Before heading for the small island, the two youths called Ambassador Kriegler from the general store.

The German ambassador sounded worried. He still had not heard from the boys' father, and was sure Mr. Hardy was in trouble. Frank told him they had found the infinity sign on one of the geologists' boring cylinders, then asked just how powerful a bomb the Rabbit might be able to build.

"We've had reports that the terrorists he's working for have been making some very sophisticated arms," the ambassador replied. "In fact, we believe they're capable of turning out small nuclear bombs of tremendous power."

"Nuclear bombs?" Frank cried into the receiver loud enough to attract the attention of several people in the store. He hushed his voice. "You mean those cylinders could be . . . ?"

The ambassador's tone was serious. "As I said, I wouldn't put anything past him. I also think it's time to get federal agents on this case. You boys have been running a terrible risk."

The older Hardy pleaded with Kriegler to give them a couple more days, explaining that they had already established a cover and were on the way to solving the mystery.

"One day is all I'll give you," the ambassador replied. "Then I'll have to turn this case over to the United States government."

Frank hung up the phone. Then, remembering something, he picked it up again and began to dial. "I forgot to call Detective Barnes," he told Joe while cupping his hand over the receiver. "He must be wondering what happened to us."

"Where in the world are you boys?" came the police detective's irritated voice over the receiver. "I let you go with the understanding you would help me with the diamond theft. The next thing I know, you're off chasing geologists, and you don't even bother to call with your whereabouts. I don't want to remind you again that all three of you are still under suspicion."

"I'm sorry," Frank said soothingly, "but this is the first chance we've had to call since yesterday afternoon. We're hot on the trail of our other case and we don't have much time left on it."

"Look," Barnes told the sleuth, his voice becoming weary. "This whole department is on my back for letting you leave the city. I promised the captain that you were working on the diamond theft. When he asks what you've uncovered so far, what am I supposed to say to him?"

Frank told the detective about their visit with Meg Rutlidge, their feelings about Boswell, and their suspicion that Max used a dog whistle to throw races.

"Okay, okay," Barnes said finally. "I'll look into Boswell, although it sounds crazy to me. But you two had better go back to the Rutlidge place and check up on this dog whistle theory of yours. And I mean now, or I'll have to ask you to come back to town."

Hanging up, Frank looked at his brother. "This leaves us between a rock and a hard place." He shrugged. "The ambassador is only giving us one more day before he sends in federal agents, and Barnes tells me if we don't work on the diamond case, we'll have to return to Washington."

"So we'll have to act fast," Joe concluded. "The Rutlidge place isn't far from here. If we leave now, we could be back before noon."

The sleuths put off their trip to Chapel Island and borrowed Fritz's sports car, which had been left at the village when they rented the boat the day before. Soon they were on the road toward Baltimore, figuring out ways they might be able to prove their theory about the dog whistle.

"Here we are," Joe announced, spotting the Rutlidge estate from the roadway and turning up the long drive toward the manor house.

The old butler, Wilkinson, greeted them at the door. "Max isn't here right now," he informed the sleuths in response to their questions. "If you would like to come in and wait for him, though, you are welcome to. I'll make some tea."

"Hold on," Frank urged Wilkinson as the butler

started toward the pantry. "We don't have that much time. Do you mind if we go to the stables and take a look around?"

"Go ahead," Wilkinson replied, showing them to the door.

At the stables, Frank and Joe found a dozen or more racehorses in their stalls.

"Look at this!" Joe said excitedly as he pulled a small, silver object from a peg on the wall.

Frank studied it for a second. "It's a dog whistle all right. Let's try it out."

"Hey, who are you?" a voice suddenly boomed from the other end of the stables.

Joe quickly stuffed the dog whistle in his pants pocket and turned to find a boy about his age running toward them. He was short, with straight brown hair and a thin face. In a moment, he stopped in front of Frank and Joe, told them he was the stable boy, and demanded to know what they wanted. His manner toward the visitors was haughty and condescending.

"The butler said we could come down here," Frank said coolly. "We're looking for Max."

"What for?" the stable boy asked, folding his arms and eyeing the two sleuths with an air of superiority.

Joe nudged his brother and took over. "We were

thinking of doing some riding," he told the boy. "In fact, this looks like a good horse right here." Joe motioned with his head toward a black colt.

"Max wouldn't let you ride Blue Lightning. Anyway," the boy continued with a smirk, "you guys wouldn't be able to handle him. That's a fast horse. He'd throw you in a second."

"But you're so great you could ride him with no sweat," Frank challenged the cocky youth.

"That's right!" the boy shot back, grabbing a saddle from a rack on the wall.

Frank and Joe exchanged winks as they watched the stable hand saddle up the young racehorse. Then he led Blue Lightning outside and mounted him.

"Watch this!" the stable boy shouted and gave the thoroughbred a kick.

Blue Lightning took off, galloping at full speed over the breeding farm's rolling fields. Frank and Joe watched as horse and rider rounded the far end of the pasture and started back. The stable boy was, in fact, a very good jockey, maneuvering the high-strung animal expertly across the field.

"Okay, do it now," Frank told his brother when the horse was about halfway back.

Joe lifted the dog whistle to his lips and blew. Suddenly Blue Lightning lost his stride, faltering noticeably and slowing down.

"Let's go," Frank said, looking at his watch.

They hurried from the stables, leaving the cocky jockey out in the field to wonder what had gone wrong.

"So our theory was right," Joe said, driving the red sports car back toward the yellow bluffs. "But it still beats me what it has to do with the stolen diamond."

"I don't know," Frank commented. "Let's give Barnes a call when we get back to the fishing village, though. Then we'll go to Chapel Island. The day's awasting."

A short time after the sleuths arrived at the village, they were out on the bay in the rented skiff, heading east by northeast. A light breeze made a slight ripple in the surface of the otherwise calm waters, and visibility was good but for a thin haze on the horizon.

"I think I see the island," Joe said after a while. He shaded his eyes from the sun and peered ahead.

A church steeple could be seen in the distance, as if rising out of the bay. A few minutes later the outline of the shore appeared beneath the steeple!

13 Island Hideout

The day had grown hot and humid by the time the sleuths' skiff reached the banks of Chapel Island. Joe attached the painter to a bush limb that hung over the water, and the two boys hacked their way inland through dense foliage.

"There's a road over here," Frank said after he had gone about thirty feet into the thick bushes.

A narrow dirt lane wound its way toward either end of Chapel Island. Using his penknife, Joe notched a groove in the bark of a tree, marking the spot where the skiff was tied.

"Which way do you think we should go?" the blond youth puzzled aloud, looking first in one direction, then the other.

Unable to determine which was the better way, Frank made a guess. "We can't get too lost in a place this size. Let's try this way." He then started down the road to the left, which seemed to head more toward the main body of the island.

The narrow lane followed the edge of Chapel Island, looping around the far end and continuing to the back side. Tracks in the dirt indicated that the road was used by horse and buggy, but these were the only signs of habitation the brothers could find as they walked through a forest of bushes and tall trees. The mosquitoes, which thrived in this kind of weather, were bothering them now and then, but it was bearable.

On the far side of the island, Frank and Joe came across a cemetery. In it were several dozen gravestones dating back to the 1700s. Curiously, many of the names on the markers were either Stone or Levenston, with few exceptions.

Joe stooped to inspect a monument dated 1706. "This looks like the oldest one here," he said. "Samuel B. Levenston. Could have been the first settler."

"Thou art wrong!" hailed a voice from the roadway.

The sleuths, who had been too busy looking over the graves to notice a horse and buggy coming down the road, now stood up as a man in simple black clothes and hat addressed them. He had dark, bushy eyebrows and a sharply chiseled nose.

"Jacob F. Stone was the first man to settle here," the stranger continued, pointing to another grave which was dated 1712. "Samuel Levenston was but the first to pass away upon this isle."

With that, the man's bushy eyebrows furrowed and he regarded the visitors with interest. "Now tell me," he said. "Why doest thou come here? And where art thou going?"

Taken aback by the buggy rider's odd blend of early English and modern dialect, Frank and Joe stood mute for a few seconds before answering. Finally, Frank spoke. "We would like to visit the island church. Are you going that way?"

"Verily, there is but one road. And to the church it leads," answered the man. "Come, I will carry thee hence." He made room for the two boys on the buggy seat.

Once aboard, Frank and Joe introduced themselves.

"And I am Jeremiah Stone," the driver answered. He chucked the reins and his horse started slowly down the road. "We have few strangers come to our island. May I ask what brings thee here?"

"We're looking for some men who might be here," said Joe. "They would also be strangers, possibly posing as oystermen."

Jeremiah Stone looked questioningly at his passengers. "Would these men be friends of thine?"

"Not at all," Frank said quickly. "We have reason to believe they're part of a dangerous gang of terrorists."

The driver frowned. "Mainlanders always bring trouble with them. Yes, I have read about terrorists in the newspapers. Methinks the world is now a very sinful place indeed."

"Is that why you speak early English and drive a horse and buggy instead of a car, to escape the modern world?" Frank queried with a hint of challenge in his voice.

Jeremiah Stone's voice rose in reply. "Ye think our community backward and stupid? We want no part of thine evil world. We choose to live here in peace as did our forefathers. But still trouble comes. Terrorists! I hope thee finds thy terrorists and begone."

"If you help us, we will be gone soon," Frank said calmly. "Have any other strangers been here recently that you know of?"

The man's disposition softened. "It is true there is a newcomer. He too, like all mainlanders, is unfriendly and Godless. He hides in his cottage, does not attend church, not even on the Sabbath. Some of us have tried to befriend him, but he will not be swayed."

"Can you take us to him?" Joe asked.

"If thou wisheth," Jeremiah responded.

Turning a corner in the dirt road, the boys found themselves entering a small community. Old Victorian houses, decorated with gingerbread latticework, clustered about a wooden church. White picket fences lined the unpaved street. Women wearing calico dresses and carrying parasols strolled by. Men wore clothing similar to Jeremiah's. They watched the young visitors with curiosity, tipping their hats at the buggy.

"Most of the tombstones in the graveyard have the names Stone or Levenston on them," Frank remarked. "Are the people living here direct descendants of those original settlers?"

"Many are indeed," Jeremiah answered. "Jacob F. Stone is my great-great-great-grandfather's grandfather, and most of those thou seest are related to either him or Samuel Levenston."

"Isn't there danger of too much inbreeding?" Joe asked.

"The church sees to it that we are in no such danger," Jeremiah answered defensively. "We have been careful to bring new blood to our community by marrying outsiders. But the newcomers must choose to live according to our heritage."

As the man spoke, he used less and less of the old English. It became clear that the church played a very strong role in the survival of the island community, and that the English they spoke was more the result of following the language in the Bible than it was of carrying it on from previous generations. This made the sleuths wonder all the more about the meaning of the signals that might well have come from the church steeple.

Jeremiah stopped in front of a cottage at the edge of town. The lawn was overgrown with weeds, and a television antenna stood on the roof.

"The newcomer lives here," Jeremiah announced. "He hides away and watches television, an evil machine which we who live here shun. His name is Jonathan Welsh."

Frank and Joe noted that none of the other houses had antennas.

"Why did he come here if not to share your way of life?" Frank wondered aloud.

"I do not know his reasons. He just arrived one day with his pockets overflowing with money and bought the house. Many of us did not want him here, but we needed money for supplies from the mainland. Now methinks it was a grave mistake."

The two sleuths went to the front door of the cottage and knocked, but no one answered. The sound of a radio or television was faintly audible. They knocked again without success, then Frank yelled Mr. Welsh's name through the closed door.

"Let's get out of here," Joe urged, afraid that the man in the cottage might be concocting an unpleasant surprise for the young detectives. "That might be the Rabbit in there, or worse."

"I thought of that," Frank said. "But I doubt he would want to blow a cover he went to such lengths to make just to get rid of us. I suggest we ask Jeremiah to see if he can lure him out. He may have more luck."

Jeremiah agreed to try convincing the cottage's occupant to open up. Frank and Joe hid in some nearby bushes where they could see the front door clearly. In a couple of minutes, Jeremiah had talked the new island resident into opening the door just wide enough to stick his head out.

"Well, he's not the Rabbit," Frank whispered. "But he still could be part of the gang."

Joe stared intently at the face in the door. Then he snapped his fingers. "That man is Arthur Rutlidge! Remember that picture of him hanging on the wall of his estate?"

"Yes!" Frank exclaimed under his breath. "So he's not dead at all. That whole boating accident was a fake!"

Both boys sprang from the bushes and ran toward the cottage. Seeing them coming, Rutlidge slammed the door.

"Mr. Rutlidge!" Joe yelled through the door. "We

know it's you in there. Whatever you're afraid of, we have nothing to do with it."

After a short pause, the wealthy horse breeder spoke from behind the door. "Who sent you here?"

"We weren't sent by anyone," Frank answered.

"Then how do you know who I am?"

Frank explained that the diamond Rutlidge had willed to the museum had been stolen, and that they had come across Rutlidge's photo during their investigation of the theft. "We also believe your trainer, Max, was involved in throwing those races," Frank added, hoping the information would inspire Rutlidge to let them in.

The horse breeder opened the door. "Come in," he said anxiously, motioning to Jeremiah and the Hardys.

Once they were inside, Arthur Rutlidge quickly shut the door. He took Jeremiah aside and spoke in a threatening whisper, making him promise not to mention what he had overheard to anyone. The island resident nodded and departed.

Arthur Rutlidge turned toward Frank and Joe. "What's this about my diamond being stolen? And how did you find me here? What do you want?"

"First tell us why you faked that boating accident and went into hiding," Frank replied directly. "Did it have something to do with the Faith diamond?"

Rutlidge looked nervous. He had lost weight

since his picture with the horse had been taken. He also appeared tired and worn, like a hunted man who couldn't sleep at night. "I had to do it," he said slowly. "My life was threatened because of the diamond."

"So you changed your will and pretended to have the boating accident," Frank put in.

"That's correct. My sister, Meg, was to have the gem. But to protect her and the diamond, I willed it to the Smithsonian, where I thought it would be safe until I came from hiding and could reclaim it. I had suspected that the races were purposely thrown. Once people thought I was dead, I hoped the culprit would expose himself by being careless."

"We think he did," Frank said, and explained how Max had probably used the dog whistle when he had taken the boys riding. "As soon as we realized your trainer blew the whistle to throw our horses, the rest fell into place."

Rutlidge nodded. "So that's how it was done." Then his expression changed and he looked keenly at his guests. "Still, I would like to know how you tracked me here."

"There was a team of geologists in the museum the day the diamond was stolen," Joe said, watching the horse breeder for his reaction. "In following them for other reasons, we stumbled on you. Quite a coincidence, don't you agree?"

Frank took up the questioning. "Maybe you aren't telling us all you know."

Rutlidge flinched, then regained his composure. "I can't tell you any more than I already have." He sat up, having heard something on the television in the next room. "Come with me."

The brothers followed Rutlidge to the den. A horserace was being broadcast over the set.

"One of my horses is in this race. Number seven, Faith," he said as they sat down.

"The one you named after the diamond to disprove the curse," Joe observed.

"Yes. Since I am not dead, the gem actually still belongs to me and not the Smithsonian. When I come out from hiding, it will be clear that the stone's powers are a hoax, that it belonged to me all along, and that my horse ran well in spite of it."

"Providing Faith does run well," Frank cautioned. "And providing the diamond is recovered."

The race began. Faith had a slow start and was several lengths behind the leaders as they came into the initial turn. By the time the horses were halfway down the first stretch, however, Faith had moved up into the pack and was gaining slowly. Rutlidge clenched his fist, urging his horse on as she rounded the far turn and broke outside to challenge the leader. The finish was neck to neck, with Faith taking it by a nose!

Rutlidge shot out of his seat and clapped his hands. "Just wait till they find out I'm still alive! They'll eat their words about that diamond causing my horses to lose. I'll get Max and Jensen behind bars before they know what hit them!"

Frank jumped up from his chair. "Did you say Jensen?" he exclaimed in surprise.

14 The Swarm

Rutlidge blinked, opened his mouth to say something, then stopped. "I . . . I've told you enough already," he murmured at last. "For your own good, drop this investigation right now. It isn't safe here!"

"Is Wayne Jensen behind all this?" the older Hardy brother persisted. "Did he try to force you into selling the stone by purposely bringing on your misfortune?"

"I think you boys ought to leave," the horse breeder said sharply. Then he sank wearily back in his chair. "Go back home."

Seeing they would get no further with the frightened man, Frank and Joe left.

"He sure is worried about something," Joe said as

they walked down the dirt road toward the church.

"Being cooped up like that can drive a guy nuts after a while," Frank said. "But it makes me wonder whether the Rabbit has more targets than just us."

Arriving at the Chapel Island church, the brothers found the minister and questioned him about recent visits from strangers. If the flashing signals had come from the steeple belfry, he might have seen something.

The aging cleric's mouth bent down at the corners. " 'Tis an interesting thing thou asks, for a man who is a stranger to mine eyes has of late joined our evening services. A crude man he is, but I be pleased that he came amongst us to find peace with God. I only hope it is not too late," the minister added, shaking his head. "Doest thou know this man?"

"His name wouldn't be Jonathan Welsh, would it?" Frank asked, referring to the name Rutlidge had used to conceal his identity.

The minister shook his head. "No. I have visited Mr. Welsh. He is a good man. I can see that quite easily. But he is deathly afraid of something he will not speak of."

"Too afraid even to go to church?" Joe questioned.

"Afraid even to leave his cottage," the minister

answered. "Do you boys know something of his troubles?"

"Yes," Frank told him. "And whoever the stranger is who attends your evening services may be part of the problem. Do you have any idea where he lives?"

The minister told them the man had come from Mosquito Island, a low and marshy place that was inhabited only by oystermen during the cooler months of the year, when oysters were in season.

"I was surprised anyone would be there in the summer months," the cleric continued. "The little island swarms with mosquitoes. A soul could be gobbled up by the devilish creatures. One hardly can believe they are God's creation."

Thanking the minister for his help, the brothers left the old church. They followed the dirt road to their skiff, which was still tied to the branch where they had left it.

"I envy those people in a way," Joe commented as he got the outboard motor running and propelled the boat away from the island. "No worries about the modern world with all its problems."

"Don't kid yourself." Frank chuckled. "There were plenty of troubles a hundred years ago, too. Now we just have different kinds."

Following the shore, the boys rounded Chapel

Island. On the far side, another island appeared, lower and smaller than the one they had just visited.

"That must be Mosquito Island," said Joe, angling the craft away from shore.

"And there's the oyster boat!" Frank cried.

The same boat that had delivered the cylinders to the geologists emerged from a winding channel leading into the island. Joe throttled the outboard and sped off in the direction of the boat. The men aboard were looking out into the bay, away from the skiff, and the boys approached the oyster boat from the rear. Once the skiff was within fifty feet of the slow-moving craft, Joe gave it full throttle.

"Let's see their reaction when we pass them," he said. "Maybe it'll give us some clue as to what they're up to now."

When they heard the outboard, the phony oystermen looked back. Suddenly, they swung their boat hard to the left.

"Hold on!" Joe shouted to his brother as he turned the skiff abruptly to avoid hitting the boat broadside.

SMACK!!

The skiff swiped the side of the larger vessel. Both boys were thrown overboard as it flipped from the impact. By the time they had gathered their senses, they were in the water and the oyster boat was on its way across the bay.

Both Hardys were excellent swimmers. They made it back to the overturned skiff, then maneuvered it toward the nearby island by paddling and kicking.

"That wasn't the best idea we've had all day," Frank said wryly as they pushed the skiff up on a sandy beach.

"There wasn't much time to think of a better plan," his brother answered. "I just hope I can get this motor to work. It took in a lot of water."

Frank gazed beyond the beach. Mosquito Island seemed nothing more than scrubby bushes and marsh. Yet, the oyster boat had come from a marked channel. Somewhere up that channel had to be a landing. "I'm going to do some exploring," the dark-haired boy announced.

While Joe tried to clear the bay water from the outboard's fuel line, Frank worked his way inland, hoping to find the oystermen's base of operation. Within a few minutes, however, he came bounding back through the marsh at a full clip, waving wildly at the air around him.

"What happened?" Joe cried in alarm.

Without answering, Frank hurtled past his brother and dove headlong into the water. A moment passed before his head popped up again. "Mosquitoes," he sputtered. "I thought they'd eat me alive!"

Joe couldn't hold down his laughter. "I thought you had seen a ghost!" he bellowed, then doubled up in laughter again at the thought of his usually composed brother running like a madman from an army of mosquitoes.

Frank, although covered with bites, had to smile himself. "Okay, okay," he said at last. "That's enough. What about the motor?"

Joe's grin left his face. "I'll need tools to get it working, and they're back at the camp. Luckily, though, I found oars wedged under the seat. At least we can row back."

Taking turns at the oars, the sleuths made their way toward camp.

As the bluffs drew closer, Frank pointed ahead. "Doesn't that look like a 'V' to you?"

Joe stopped rowing and gazed at the face of the bluff. A huge letter "V" was cut in the yellow clay, extending from the top of the cliff almost to the water. "One of those grooves must have been what we used to climb down to the beach last night," he deduced. "What do you think it means?"

"Maybe it's the Roman numeral for five, or 'V' for victory," Frank guessed.

Stumped by the purpose of the huge letter, the boys continued rowing. By the time they arrived at camp, the sun had set. They were both sunburned and exhausted, and hoped Chet had a meal waiting for them. Neither Chet nor Fritz, however, was there.

"They were supposed to wait for us," Joe said anxiously.

Frank went to the tent and got a flashlight. He scanned the beach until the flashlight's beam landed on two sets of tracks leading away from camp. No unfamiliar footprints or signs of a scuffle were visible. "At least they left camp at their own will," he declared. "We'd better follow their tracks in any case."

Summoning their last reserves of energy, the tired sleuths jogged down the beach in search of their companions.

Suddenly, Frank turned off his flashlight and motioned for his brother to stop. In the darkness, someone was running toward them!

15 Kidnapped!

"Frank! Joe!" the figure hollered in a German accent.

"It's Fritz!" Joe shouted, running to meet him.

"Are you all right?" Frank asked the ambassador's son when the three of them were together.

"I think they got Chet!" Fritz gasped.

"Who got him?" Joe cried.

Fritz took a few seconds to catch his breath. "We . . . we were watching the geologists. The oyster boat came again, so we tried to get a closer look. They spotted us. I got away, but they must have captured Chet."

"Let's go!" Frank commanded his brother.

Leaving Fritz, who was too exhausted to run any

farther, Frank and Joe took off down the beach. They reached the geologists' drilling site to find the oyster boat gone and no one around. Without stopping, they scaled the bluff and ran along the road until they arrived at Dr. Werner's bungalow.

The pickup truck was parked outside. Inside, two men were roughly interrogating the geologist. Frank and Joe moved closer to the window. The Doberman was tied to a couch. The dog snarled and barked as one of the men, Roget, slapped Werner across the face. He was demanding something of the German, and threatening that he would put an end to him. The second man busily ransacked the house, pulling out drawers and ripping through furniture.

"The Rabbit," Frank murmured, identifying the man as the albino terrorist.

"Now's our chance," Joe said eagerly.

The brothers burst through the front door. Caught off guard, Roget and the Rabbit were struck by Frank and Joe's fists before they were able to react. But they recovered in an instant to return the punches.

"You two will pay for this!" the terrorist spat as he prepared to strike Frank again.

Frank ducked the Rabbit's fist and landed a stiff upper cut squarely on the man's jaw. The terrorist flew back against a chair, dizzied by the blow. Frank got ready to pounce, but the Rabbit quickly jumped up and hoisted the chair above his head.

Meanwhile, Joe was still exchanging blows with Roget, but was beginning to lose the upper hand in the fight.

Just then, the Doberman broke from its leash and lunged at the Rabbit. The terrorist brought the chair down heavily on the ferocious dog. It yelped with pain as the wood splintered against its back, but it only became more vicious as a result and lunged again. The Rabbit dodged the beast and ran for the door. Roget followed. In a few seconds, the two men were tearing out of the driveway in the pickup truck.

Werner, who had left the room during the fight, returned and calmed the excited animal.

"Where were you?" Frank said angrily to the geologist. "We could have used your help."

"You made a mistake in coming here," the bearded man spoke evenly. "I was in no danger."

"No danger?" Joe cried in disbelief. "Those two guys had it in for you! Do you know who that albino man is?"

"Yes. And I also know who you are. You are Joe Hardy and that is your brother Frank."

The brothers were stunned by the geologist's words. Finally, Frank spoke. "If you know who we are, maybe you can tell us what happened to our friend Chet."

"Or what happened to our father," Joe put in sharply.

The scientist's eyes narrowed. "I warned you to stay out of this and you did not listen."

"*You* warned us?" cried Joe. "When did . . . ?" Suddenly, he remembered the mysterious phone call they had received in Bayport. The man had spoken with a thick German accent. "You called us," he said, snapping his fingers.

Werner nodded. "If you had taken my advice, your friend would not be in trouble."

Joe made a move to grab the geologist, but stopped as the Doberman bared its teeth in warning.

"The Rabbit will be back," Werner went on. "Now I hope you are impressed that you should not be meddling. You know too much as it is. Your father and your friend will not be safe if you insist on pursuing this further."

"Look," Frank said, taking a step toward the geologist. "The federal government will be sending men down here tomorrow unless we give them a reason not to. So you had better cooperate with us. We saw the infinity sign on those boring cylinders and we know what they are."

145

Werner stared at Frank, not sure whether to believe his story. "I will tell you where your friend is," he said at last. "But I cannot tell you any more. You may call these government men if you wish, but remember, your father's safety is at stake. If you value his life, you will ask the government to stay away."

"Where's Chet?" Joe demanded.

"He is being held captive on Mosquito Island, several miles—"

"We know where it is," Joe said.

While Joe stayed with the geologist, trying to pry more information from him, Frank went into a back room of the bungalow and called the ambassador. Kriegler agreed to hold off sending in federal agents unless he did not hear from the boys by the following afternoon.

He was shocked to learn that Dr. Werner was involved with the terrorists. "The man has an excellent reputation," he said. "I can't believe he would do anything wrong."

"He might have been forced into cooperating with the gang," Frank said. "There's something very strange about this whole thing."

"I know," Kriegler said. "And it worries me that you have no help down there. Be extra careful, will you?"

Frank promised, then hung up and went back

into the living room. Joe had not had any success in shedding more light on the mystery. Werner's dog stood guard in the corner, ready to spring if the boys made a move toward his master.

"Come on," Frank said to his brother. "Let's find Chet."

The two sleuths left the bungalow and walked toward camp. On the way, Frank related his conversation with Kriegler.

"I'm glad he's holding off for another day," Joe said. "I just hope we can crack this case in the next twenty-four hours!"

"First thing we have to do is to find Chet," Frank decided, "and before we do, we have to fix the outboard and get a few hours' rest."

Back in their tent, the two exhausted youths fell asleep instantly. But by the first light of dawn, Frank and Joe were up and working on the skiff's motor. Fritz made a quick breakfast for them, and soon they were on their way in the gray morning light, heading east by northeast, while the ambassador's son remained to spy on the geologists.

The water wasn't as calm as it had been the day before. The wind had picked up and the small skiff bounced over choppy seas.

"If this gets any rougher," Frank called from the bow, "our boat won't be able to handle it. She's getting shaky as it is."

The wind increased and a line of dark clouds appeared on the horizon, moving rapidly down the bay in the direction of the boys.

"I'm going back to shore," Joe said, uneasy over the approaching storm. He swung the boat around. "We'd better wait this thing out."

As the skiff headed toward the bluffs, the wind and waves grew in force. Soon the storm was almost overhead. As the cliffs drew near, the brothers could make out someone scraping letters in the yellow clay with a shovel.

"That's Fritz!" Joe yelled. "He's writing something!"

The boys watched intently as Fritz's message became clear. BOMB it said in bold letters.

"Bomb?" Frank exclaimed. "He must be trying to warn us!"

Frank and Joe looked up and down the beach for any sign of the Rabbit. When they brought the skiff closer, Fritz waved his arms, frantically motioning for them to get away. But the storm was almost upon them!

Suddenly, something landed in the water near the skiff and exploded.

Kaboom!

16 Stormy Crossing

A column of water shot in the air, nearly swamping the small boat.

"Up there!" Joe hollered, as he pointed toward the top of the looming yellow bluffs.

Standing on the cliff's edge, silhouetted against the stormy sky, was the Rabbit. He hurled one small bomb after the next from his perch high above the two youths, who bobbed like sitting ducks in the rough waters.

"Let's get out of here!" Frank urged as another bomb barely missed their bow.

Giving it full throttle, Joe swung the skiff around. The bombs hit the water like a barrage of mortar shells, and he had to zigzag away from the shore to make a difficult target for the Rabbit.

By the time the sleuths were out of range of the terrorist's assault, dense, black clouds had rolled in overhead, bringing strong winds and a heavy rain with them.

"Hold her into the wind!" Frank shouted.

"I'm trying!" Joe answered, knowing he must direct the small craft into the oncoming waves to prevent it from being capsized.

But the waves, driven by the whistling gale, had grown too short and too steep to keep the skiff's nose angled at them. Frank searched the compartments under the seats for life jackets, but either the boat wasn't supplied with them or they had been lost in the encounter with the oystermen.

"Take her back in," Frank ordered.

"What about the Rabbit?" Joe cried, his clothes soaked with rain. "He'll be waiting for us."

Frank hesitated, unsure of his decision. The waves and wind grew with each second. "Take her ashore," he repeated at last.

A bolt of lightning shot from the dark sky, for a fraction of a second illuminating the wet, frightened faces of the two youths. Joe turned the skiff back toward the bluffs, now barely visible through the driving rain.

"I'll head her downwind," he said, hoping they could lose the Rabbit by landing farther along the shore under cover of the storm.

Again lightning lit up the sky. For an instant, the

sleuths could make out the figure at the top of the bluffs. The terrorist walked along the cliff's edge, steadily following the skiff as it moved down the coast. Joe imagined he saw the Rabbit grin, as if pleased by this game of cat and mouse.

"Watch out!" Frank screamed, warning his brother of an oncoming wave that threatened to swamp the tiny boat.

Joe's attention left the bluffs as he made a desperate effort to avoid the wave. But it was too late. The skiff was caught by its stern and turned on its end with an abrupt twist. A second later, both boys found themselves in the water. Their boat was quickly swallowed up by the churning seas.

Desperately, the young sleuths tried to swim toward shore. But the driving waves and wind were against them, and washed them even further into the stormy bay.

Just then, seemingly out of nowhere, a boat appeared, crashing through the waves in the direction of the helpless youths. It was an old, wooden sloop with a single raked mast. Frank and Joe yelled and waved at the approaching vessel. When it was close enough, the skipper threw a line with a life ring attached to the end. "Hold tight!" he yelled from aboard the sloop as the brothers grabbed the life ring.

Wet and shivering, they were soon pulled onto the boat's deck by a sturdy old man in a yellow rain slicker. "Go below and dry yourselves," he ordered.

Joe started to thank him for saving them, but the sailor interrupted by repeating his command. Then he returned to the sloop's tiller without another word.

In the boat's cabin, the boys found towels and blankets. Removing their wet clothes, they wrapped themselves in the blankets and huddled below deck until the storm was over. The dark clouds rolled away as quickly as they had come, and warm sunlight greeted the youths as they emerged from the cabin.

The sloop was manned solely by the old sailor, who had removed his rain slicker. Long, white whiskers flowed from his leathery skin. "You kids were stupid to be out here in this kind of weather," he scolded. "You're very lucky I spotted you. That skiff didn't have a chance in this storm."

Frank thanked the skipper for rescuing them, and explained that they had not expected the storm would be so severe.

The man's steel gray eyes softened. "Most of the time the bay is as gentle as a pond," he said, gazing across the expanse of water. "You could sail a dinghy from one end to the other. Then, just when you think she's a piece of cake, one of these thunder-bumpers will blow down out of the north. Can hit you like a brick before you have a chance to trim your sails, and all at once it's like being caught in a big washing machine. Many a skipper has learned the hard way to have respect for these waters."

The old salt paused for a moment to let his words sink in, then continued in a lighter tone. "I've seen it raining frogs from the skies during these storms."

"Raining frogs?" Joe asked, not sure if he had heard correctly.

The sailor chuckled. "Sometimes the wind comes up so hard and fast, it picks up little frogs from the shore and blows them out in the bay. Had a few land on my deck."

Finding the story hard to swallow, Frank just nodded politely and changed the subject. "You're a crabber?" he asked, having noticed some crab pots piled in the sloop's stern.

"In the summer I am," the old man replied. "The rest of the year, I'm an oysterer. Been at it my whole life."

"Do you know Mosquito Island?" Joe queried.

The white-whiskered skipper looked curiously at his two passengers. "Spent many a year working out that way. What makes you ask?"

"We have a friend who's being held captive there," Frank said directly.

The old salt's curiosity turned to surprise as the boys explained that the island might be the headquarters for a gang of terrorists, who presently held Chet at their mercy. Without hesitation, he volunteered to take them there.

"This could well be dangerous," Frank warned. "Those men would as soon get rid of us as swat a fly."

"When you're my age, you haven't time to be scared of anyone," the skipper said with a glimmer in his eyes. "By the way, my name is Jake, and the boat's called *Marybelle*."

"Frank and Joe Hardy," Frank introduced himself and his brother.

Jake acknowledged it with a grin, then let out the sloop's sail and set course for Mosquito Island. The boys changed back to their clothes, which they had hung out on deck to dry. The wind was still fresh from the north, and the old sailing vessel made good time as it cut its way through the choppy bay waters.

"Mosquito Island is next to the island I came from," Jake told the sleuths.

"You lived on Chapel Island?" Joe asked.

"That's right. I'm descended from the original settlers."

"Are you a Stone?"

The old skipper nodded. "Jacob Stone the Sixth. How do you know about the Stones?"

Frank explained how they had visited Chapel Island the day before and met Jeremiah Stone. Then he asked why Jake had left the island.

"Wanted to get out and see the world," was the old man's reply. "I got itchy with all their talk about

155

how evil it was. Made me go and take a look for myself. I've been around the world several times on boats, and believe me, I've seen more than my share of it. Now I'm thinking of going back to the island and retiring there in peace. Only from what you boys tell me, even Chapel Island has trouble brewing on its back porch. It's a shame."

"Well, with your help," Frank said, "we might be able to put an end to it right now."

Jake sailed the sloop around Chapel Island, and the smaller, mosquito-infested island came into view.

"Take the tiller," the skipper told Frank as they approached.

Frank took control of the sloop's steering while Jake stepped down into the cabin. The old man reappeared a moment later with a bottle of greenish liquid, which he applied to his face and arms. He then handed it to his passengers. "Here, put this on. It'll keep those mosquitos from eating you alive."

The boys doused themselves liberally with the homemade insect repellent. It smelled like rotting fish.

"Phew!" Joe exclaimed at the odor. "I sure hope it works."

Rounding Mosquito Island, Jake sailed into the channel, which was lined with thick underbrush, and negotiated his way expertly along its winding course.

"There's the landing," Joe said in a hushed tone as they rounded a corner.

A run-down wooden shack and a dock were the only constructions at the landing site. The oyster boat wasn't there, and there was no sign of anyone. Noiselessly, Jake pulled up to the dock and the two sleuths hopped from the boat.

In crouched positions, Frank and Joe crept toward the wooden shack. If someone was inside, they wanted to catch him by surprise. Frank motioned for Joe to sneak behind the shack while he tried the front entrance.

After listening intently for a few minutes, Frank opened the door with a swift kick. It flew back without resistance, and he prepared to defend himself.

At first, the shack did seem to be empty. But as the young detective's eyes adjusted to the dim light, he saw three figures lying on the floor, bound and gagged. Just then Joe came back, and both boys rushed inside.

"Dad!" Joe cried out.

17 The Chase Quickens

Fenton Hardy and Chet, both bound by their wrists and ankles with heavy rope, made anxious noises through their gags. The third captive was a girl with long, chestnut brown hair. She stared at Frank and Joe with fear, not knowing whether they meant her harm or not.

"See if Jake has a knife," Frank said to his brother.

Joe ran back to the sloop while Frank quickly untied the captives' gags. Mosquito bites covered their exposed faces and arms.

"What happened? What are you doing here?" Frank asked his father, who was supposed to be in Germany.

"I'd like to know the same thing from you," the famous detective replied with a smile. "But I'm certainly glad you came. We haven't much time left. I'll tell you all about it later. Right now let's get these ropes off."

Using the sharp edge of an oyster shell he found on the floor, Frank started cutting his father's ropes. Joe returned with Jake's rigging knife, which he used to free Chet and the girl.

"Boy, I'm sure happy you guys showed up." Chet groaned as he rose to his feet. "I must have been lunch for five hundred mosquitoes!"

"Well, now you know what it's like to be the eat*ee* instead of the eater," Joe kidded his pal.

"All I know," Chet replied, swatting his arm as another mosquito prepared to dine, "is that I want to get off this island, and pronto!"

The chestnut-haired girl, realizing that the boys were there to help them escape, let out a flood of words in German. Teary-eyed, she thanked her rescuers. She seemed to be about sixteen. Joe began to question her, wondering how she became mixed up in this affair. But Mr. Hardy insisted that they make their escape without hesitation.

Hurrying from the shack, the group boarded the old sloop. Jake hoisted his sail. In a few minutes, they were back on the bay.

Mr. Hardy listened eagerly to his sons' story. "It

all seems to fit," he said, once the boys had finished recounting their adventures. "The Rabbit was hired by a terrorist organization called Vici, which means 'I conquered,' in Latin. Vici, in turn, is under contract by a Middle Eastern group involved in the illegal export of oil. The man who tried to buy the stolen diamond from you, Wayne Jensen, is the American connection for the Middle Eastern organization."

The young detectives seemed puzzled. "But why does Jensen want the diamond?" Frank asked.

"And what is the gang doing here?" Joe added. "And why are the geologists involved?"

Frank frowned. "Wait a minute. You say Jensen is involved in oil dealings, Dad?"

Mr. Hardy nodded.

"I wonder if there's a nuclear power plant near Yellow Clay Cliffs," Frank went on.

"As a matter of fact, there is," Mr. Hardy replied. "It's a couple of miles west of the cliffs."

"That's it!" Frank cried out. "I think I know what that gang is up to!"

Joe and Mr. Hardy caught on the same instant.

"You mean they're fabricating earthquakes to sabotage nuclear power plants in order to further their oil interests?" Joe asked his brother.

"It's possible," Mr. Hardy said. "I learned that the terrorists were actively producing small and powerful nuclear bombs, but I didn't know for what purpose. I was on the gang's trail when they transported the bombs to a waiting freighter on the coast of Spain. Unfortunately, I was captured while attempting to save this young lady from being kidnapped aboard the ship. I was then taken on the same freighter myself, where I was kept prisoner until we arrived here a little over a week ago."

"Do you know who the girl is?" Frank asked.

"No. But I overheard the men saying that the last piece of the bomb was being taken to Yellow Clay Cliffs today, and that the whole thing would be over by this evening."

"But if the gang is causing the earthquakes with the bombs, what is Dr. Werner's part in this?" Joe spoke up.

Just then the German girl, who had been trying to understand what she could of the conversation, became excited. "Werner!" She exclaimed. Speaking in her native tongue, she told them that she was Katerina Werner, Dr. Hasso Werner's daughter. She had been kidnapped from her home in Germany while her father was working on a geology project in the United States.

Joe snapped his fingers. "That explains why Dr. Werner got mixed up with the terrorists! They forced him into serving them by kidnapping his daughter!"

"It also explains why Werner wanted us to stay out of his way," Frank put in. "He was trying to protect Katerina, and he didn't want us to become victims of the Rabbit and his gang. That's why he tried warning us off the case!"

The sun began to sink below the horizon as the sloop neared the mainland shore. Jake, now almost as anxious as his passengers to apprehend the gang, steered a steady course toward the geologists' drilling site. Mr. Hardy continued to discuss the mysterious case with his sons. Katerina gazed ahead. Her thoughts were filled with worry about her father being in the clutches of the terrorists, who might try to dispose of him once their mission was completed.

"We'll be getting there before long if this wind keeps up," the old sailor said, judging their distance from the yellow cliffs.

Frank stood up and surveyed the approaching shore. But they were still too far out in the bay for him to see any signs of activity on the beach.

"How did you come upon the information about the meeting at the Smithsonian?" he asked his father as he sat down again.

Mr. Hardy grinned. "I discovered some communication between two members of the terrorist ring," he replied. "At the time, I didn't know what it meant, or else I would have given you more specific instructions. Shortly afterward, I was captured. I'm glad the message got to you through Ambassador Kriegler, even though it was a dangerous mission."

"We've had some close calls," Frank admitted. "And it looks as if we still have a rough time ahead of us. If the Rabbit means to use his bomb tonight, none of us are safe by a long shot."

"We also left the ambassador's son, Fritz, in a bad spot," Joe put in.

The detective appeared thoughtful. "Our only hope is to catch the men before they have a chance to carry out their plan," he declared. "We should also contact Kriegler as soon as possible. We're outnumbered by those in the gang, and Kriegler might be able to get his men down here in time to pitch in. Werner may also be of great help to us once he finds out his daughter is safe."

When their father had finished speaking, Frank and Joe stationed themselves at the sloop's bow. Night had fallen as they drew near the beach. The oyster boat was not there, and the site was abandoned. The drilling equipment had been removed! Jake ran his boat up on the sand, and his passengers climbed out.

"We're too late!" Chet moaned, seeing that the cylinders were gone as well.

"We'll have to warn the power plant," Mr. Hardy

declared. "And we'll have to catch those crooks. If the Rabbit can set this bomb, he may also be able to deactivate it. We'll have to act fast!"

"I can get you to the power plant," Jake volunteered. "My place is just a short trip up the coast and I have my car there."

All except Frank and Joe returned to the sloop.

"I'll contact Kriegler from the power plant," Mr. Hardy called to his sons as he boarded the boat. "Do what you can to find those men. But be careful!"

The brothers turned and began to scale the steep path up the bluff face. Once up to the clay cliff road, they ran in the direction of Werner's bungalow.

18 Night Rendezvous

The lights were out in the geologist's house. But the pickup truck was in the driveway, and another car was parked next to it.

"A gray Peugeot," Frank muttered. "I bet that's the car that trailed Fritz and Chet to the dock!"

"But where are the men?" Joe asked, puzzled. "They didn't leave their truck so they could hike their way out of this wilderness!"

"No," his brother agreed. "They must be around somewhere."

The two stopped in their tracks, not knowing in which direction to go. The night was calm, the only sound the constant chirp of crickets and the washing of waves on the beach far below.

"The oyster boat," said Frank in a hushed tone. "It wasn't at the island or the drilling site. Maybe that's how they're making their getaway!"

The boys hurried to the edge of the bluff and looked out over the dark water.

"We lost them," Joe cried in frustration. "They probably went back to the island to pick up their hostages. I bet we went right by those creeps on our way here."

"Ships passing in the night," Frank reflected, searching the water below them with his eyes.

"Hey, look!" Joe said suddenly. He pointed at the horizon, where a light flashed dimly in the distance. "Signals from Chapel Island again. Maybe that's where they are!"

"You could be right," Frank said, growing excited. "Arthur Rutlidge might be part of this thing after all. Also, those signals mean at least someone is still over here to communicate with."

The brothers all at once sensed that they might not be alone on the bluff. They drew away from the cliff's edge to some bushes on the other side of the road, listening intently.

The light repeated its signal at short intervals, as if expecting responding flashes. The boys kept their eyes open for an answer from their side of the bay. But the signal continued with no response.

Frank nudged his younger brother. "Doesn't it

look like Morse code, three short flashes and one long one?"

Familiar with the old method used to send messages by telegraph, Joe watched as the signal repeated itself. "Yes," he said at last with a nod. "In Morse code it would stand for the letter 'V.' Do you think that could have something to do with the 'V' we saw on the face of the bluff?"

"Not just that," the older boy answered. "Remember what Dad said? The terrorists' organization is called Vici. That could be their pickup signal, and the 'V' on the bluff could be the pickup point."

"I've got an idea," Joe said after a short pause. "Come on, hurry!"

The two sleuths returned to Werner's bungalow. In less than a minute, Joe had the geologists' truck hot-wired, and they drove it out of the driveway onto the bluff road. Stopping on the promontory where Roget had signaled with his headlights, Joe flashed out the letter "V" in Morse code. They could see an answer in the distance and noticed that the signal became increasingly brighter and clearer, as if the source was getting closer.

"Wait a second," breathed Joe. "Those flashes are coming from a boat, not Chapel Island. Someone out there thinks we're the gang, and is about to pick us up!"

Frank looked at his brother. "That's great, but

what do you plan to do when they get here?"

"I don't know," Joe answered. "I just hope Dad brings help soon."

The sleuths watched as the boat drew closer. Their father and the federal agents would not arrive for a while, so they climbed down the cliff to the beach, hoping the darkness would somehow make it possible for them to take advantage of the situation. But they were still without a plan.

Suddenly, a voice spoke up behind them. "What are you doing here?"

The boys wheeled around. Dr. Werner stepped out of the shadows, glaring at them. "How many times do I have to tell you to stay out of this?" he cried out. "You have no idea what danger you are causing for yourselves and others."

"Your daughter Katerina is safe, sir," Frank told him quickly.

The geologist's jaw dropped and his eyes grew wide. "My—my daughter? What are you talking about?"

"Your daughter was being held captive on Mosquito Island with our father and our friend," Frank continued. "We rescued her and she's now with our dad at the power plant to warn them of the upcoming nuclear explosion. Do you still want us to stay out of this?"

Overcome with relief, Werner nearly fainted. In a moment, however, he composed himself and thanked the boys. "What can I do to show you my gratitude?" he asked.

"You can help us capture the men who put you up to this," Joe told him. "A boat should be arriving here soon and we'll need your help to get aboard."

"Yes, I know. I will gladly help," the German geologist replied.

Just then the boat, which had been giving the "V" signal, appeared out of the night, coming toward the beach at a rapid pace.

"It's Jensen's yacht!" Joe cried, recognizing the sixty-foot cabin cruiser.

Werner waved as the large boat's spotlight scanned the beach. Frank and Joe ducked behind a log lying in the sand. The spotlight beam rested on the geologist, and the yacht slowed as it eased its way into the landing spot at the beach. A boarding ladder was thrown from the bow by a deckhand. Werner started up the ladder and reached out for the sailor to pull him aboard.

Then, with a quick yank, he grabbed the man's hand and pulled him over the side. At the same moment, the two young sleuths jumped from behind the log. Before the deckhand could yell for help, they knocked him out. Then Frank and Joe boarded the yacht behind Werner. They quickly overcame a second man on their way to the cabin. When they threw open the door, they found a startled Wayne Jensen at the yacht's controls.

Jensen shot an acid glance at Frank and Joe, then stared at the geologist. "So you decided to double-cross us, eh, Werner?" he said maliciously. "You know what will happen to your daughter if you don't cooperate."

Werner's eyes became slits. "Tie him up," he said to the Hardys, then pushed Jensen aside and took control of the yacht himself.

Finding spare rope in a storage compartment, the sleuths bound the struggling oilman's hands and feet. Werner backed the sixty-foot yacht away from the beach and turned it around.

"Where are the others?" Frank asked the geologist.

"Probably on Mosquito Island," Werner replied. "Jensen was going to pick them up first, then come by and get me. I don't know why they changed their plan."

Joe explained that they had signaled Jensen from the bluff.

"Very clever," Jensen sneered, struggling with his ropes. "But I'm afraid you're a little late for the big coup."

Frank looked anxiously from Jensen to Werner,

remembering that the bomb was probably soon to go off. "Are we too late?" he asked.

The geologist sighed. "I hope not. I will explain everything, but right now there's a signal being given to us ahead."

Werner steered the yacht toward a light that flashed the "V" code. It came from the direction of Mosquito Island.

"We're expecting help at the drilling site soon," Frank said. "If we can get the gang on board and take them there, we'll be all right."

Werner glanced at the sleuths. "That may not be such an easy trick. When those men find their hostages missing, they will be very angry, and very suspicious, especially the Rabbit." The geologist switched on the yacht's searchlight. "There they are now, on the oyster boat."

The craft was just off the small island. It carried not only the albino terrorist, but Werner's entire team.

"Those men aren't really geologists, are they?" Joe said to Werner.

"No. They're members of the Vici terrorist gang," Dr. Werner answered bitterly. "I'm the only real geologist among them. The big one, Roget, is their leader."

As the yacht made ready to intercept the oyster boat, the sleuths gagged Jensen. Frank put on the oilman's captain's hat and jacket, then took the controls while Werner went forward to assist the men aboard. Joe crouched in the corner of the cabin, ready to spring if anyone tried to enter.

Soon the two boats met.

"Where's my Katerina?" Werner said angrily to Roget, pretending to be upset that his daughter was not on the boat. "It is over now and you must return her to me."

Roget stepped up on the yacht's deck. "We will give her back only after the Rabbit has received his payment," he lied, as if the girl were still in their clutches. "We have hidden her."

Following Roget came the Rabbit. His white hair and pinkish skin appeared ghostlike in the moonlight. "I will receive my payment tonight," he hissed threateningly to Werner. His pink eyes shifted about, focusing only for an instant on the geologist. "If I am not satisfied, your precious daughter will die!"

19 Delicate Cargo

"You've said enough," Werner interrupted the terrorist. "I will see to it that you are given what you deserve."

The Rabbit mumbled something under his breath as he turned from the geologist, watching the rest of the men climb on deck and file into the yacht's stateroom. Only a short hallway and a door separated the terrorists from the sleuths in the control cabin.

All was quiet while Frank put the cruiser in gear and headed toward the bluffs, where he hoped Mr. Hardy would be waiting with the federal agents. The oyster boat was left drifting in the bay.

Suddenly, the door leading from the stateroom to

the control cabin opened part way. Dr. Werner's voice could be heard from the other side.

"He will discuss it with you later," the geologist argued. "Mr. Jensen told me he doesn't want to be bothered with the subject right now."

"I have no more time to waste with either you or Jensen," the Rabbit grumbled, and the cabin door opened further.

Frank pulled his cap down, hiding his face. Joe pressed himself against the wall to one side of the door. If they could take the Rabbit quickly enough, he wouldn't have time to cry out an alarm to the others.

"Do you hear me, Mr. Jensen?" the Rabbit challenged. "I must be paid tonight, or nobody will go anywhere."

In a frantic gesture, Werner grabbed the terrorist's arm, pulling him back into the hall before he had a chance to recognize Frank. "You will get nothing until my daughter is given back to me!" the geologist shouted in a display of wild desperation. "You lying cheat! You told me Katerina would be on the oyster boat with you!"

Werner kept yelling as he wrestled the Rabbit down the hall away from the yacht's control cabin. Several minutes later, he reappeared, his jacket torn and his jaw bruised. "Well, it worked," he told the two sleuths with a grin. "Are we almost there? I don't know how much longer I can hold these people off."

"We should be arriving soon," Frank replied.

"Dad better be there with help," Joe put in anxiously.

As the huge motor yacht moved through the water, Dr. Werner and the young sleuths watched intently for the bluffs to appear out of the darkness.

"I will now explain to you what happened," the geologist told the boys in a hushed tone. "I did not know at first what the Vici gang was up to, only that they had Katerina and I was to cooperate with them. All they told me was that they were testing something underground, and that I was to be in charge of boring holes for the tests. It was not until the first earthquake that I began to understand their intentions."

"The earthquake at Bayridge?" Frank asked.

Werner nodded. "Yes. The gang had developed a small nuclear bomb in the shape of core cylinders. Its explosion caused a minor earthquake." He paused for a moment, then went on. "At that point, I became very suspicious of their plan, so I tried to listen to what was being said behind my back. It turned out they had been hired by someone to sabotage nuclear power plants and make it appear as if natural earthquakes caused the damage."

"We figured that," Frank said. "The Bayridge plant almost had a serious problem."

"We were at the facility when the quake hit," Joe added.

"Then you know what I am talking about," Werner whispered. "But that was only a test for the real show down here. The bomb that the Rabbit planted at the foot of the bluffs is three times more powerful than the one in Bayridge!"

Frank shot an accusing glance at the geologist. "And you were willing to go along with risking the lives of perhaps thousands of people to save your daughter?"

"I wanted to thwart their scheme," Werner replied solemnly. "I thought up a plan of my own. That's why I tried to prevent you boys from interfering."

Seeing the embarrassment on the youths' faces, Werner quickly added that if it had not been for them, the plan to save his daughter would not have worked.

"But the bomb has already been set," Joe said in alarm.

"It will go off," Werner told them. "But I studied the geological formation of the earth very carefully before we chose a drilling site. I misled the terrorists into believing the spot I picked would cause a

176

severe quake. In fact, however, I selected a particularly poor place to set the bomb. The earth should absorb nearly all of the explosive's power without affecting the surface to any great extent."

"Are you sure of your calculations?" Frank asked.

"Yes and no," the geologist replied tensely. "The bomb will definitely not be as strong as Vici had planned. But exactly what its effect will be is impossible to know. It is set to go off at midnight, so we'll find out shortly."

Frank glanced at his watch. It was just past eleven o'clock. The bomb would explode in less than an hour. "How did Vici expect to fool everyone with the earthquakes?" the dark-haired sleuth queried. "Geologists would soon learn that they were caused by the bombs, wouldn't they?"

"I expect they would," Werner shrugged. "But the terrorists were hoping that the mysterious quakes would take a while to investigate, giving them time to cause a number of such incidents before being found out."

"There are the bluffs!" Joe said suddenly, turning their attention. Out of the night, the yellow cliffs rose up rapidly in front of them. A cluster of figures were visible on the beach. "It must be Dad and the federal agents!" The blond-haired youth's voice cracked with excitement.

Frank headed the craft toward shore. "We'll have

to act fast," he said, taking command. "I'm going to ram her up against the beach."

The yacht slackened speed only a little as it neared the dock. Frank wanted to hit the beach with enough impact to temporarily panic the gang members. Werner went to the bow, where he would be able to shout a warning to those waiting below the cliffs.

With a crunch, the yacht smacked the piling. The terrorists, unprepared for the sudden stop, flew against the walls of the stateroom. By the time they recovered, Dr. Werner had already hopped off the boat to alert the federal agents to take cover.

"Let's get them!" Frank exclaimed, abandoning the yacht's controls. The boys ran onto the deck and, with swift blows, greeted the dazed terrorists as they filed out of the stateroom. Soon, the brothers were joined by several federal agents. The fighting on deck became heavy. Both sides were evenly matched at first, but as more agents climbed aboard, they managed to subdue the gang members.

From the corner of his eye, Frank saw one of the men creep noiselessly over the side. Almost invisible, he moved quickly across the beach and began to scale the bluff. "The Rabbit's getting away!" the older Hardy called to his brother, who was helping to handcuff one of the oyster boat operators.

Both boys took off after the albino terrorist. By the time they reached the bottom of the bluff, however, the Rabbit had already made it to the top.

"We can't lose him," Joe cried, scrambling upward as fast as he could.

Once on the yellow clay road, the sleuths raced in the direction of Werner's bungalow. They feared the Rabbit would make his escape in the gray sedan, and expected that at any second the vehicle would come speeding toward them from around a bend. But when they arrived at the house, they found themselves witness to a peculiar scene.

Fritz and Werner's Doberman had the terrorist cornered in the driveway. The boy held the dog by its leash, preventing the angry beast from pouncing upon the Rabbit.

"Makes a good rabbit dog, don't you think?" the ambassador's son told Frank and Joe with a restrained chuckle.

The Rabbit's eyes, in fact, had the wild look of a cornered animal. He glanced from Fritz to the Hardy brothers, and a fiendish grin spread over his face. "I've been waiting for you punks to show up," he sneered, then drew an object from his jacket pocket. "Now that I have all of you together, I have a little present for you."

"It's a bomb!" Joe cried.

20 Eruption

The terrorist cocked his arm to heave the bomb. Fritz let go of the ferocious dog, and before the Rabbit had time to deliver his goods, he was on the ground. Frank grabbed the bomb from the man's hand and carefully placed it some distance away. It would go off only on impact.

Pulling the Doberman off the Rabbit, the boys quickly used Joe's belt to bind the albino's hands behind his back. The cornered terrorist struggled violently, but finally realized that he was helpless against the young detectives.

"That's what's known as a quarterback sack," Frank quipped, referring to a football play in which

181

the quarterback is tackled before he has time to throw the ball.

"Right," Joe said, speaking to the now calmed dog. "You made a pretty good play."

"The game is not over yet," the Rabbit spat out.

"It's over for you," Frank replied sternly.

The three boys hoisted the man to his feet and led him down to the beach, where Mr. Hardy and the team of federal agents had the other terrorists tied together in the sand. The dog followed.

Seeing Dr. Werner and Katerina, the Doberman bounded toward them with glee. It jumped on its hind legs, and, putting its front paws on the girl's shoulders, wagged its tail and licked her in greeting.

"Stop it, Alex!" The girl giggled as she tried to avoid the animal's tongue.

Dr. Werner began to laugh too, in good spirits for the first time since Frank and Joe had met him.

Just then, Detective Barnes stepped out of the shadows. "Hi, boys. Just thought I'd come down to see what you were up to." The hazel-eyed police detective smiled.

"How did you get here?" Frank said with a puzzled expression as he shook Barnes's hand.

"Oh, I had been in touch with the ambassador,

and when he told me a little about what was going on, I decided to tag along."

The two sleuths took the detective aside to discuss the diamond theft. Barnes told them that he had followed up on the hunch they had about the curator.

"Boswell had some crazy notion that Arthur Rutlidge was still alive, and that, after giving his diamond to the museum, he then proceeded to steal it."

"I don't think he stole it," Frank said. "At least, he said he didn't."

"What do you mean he said he didn't? The man's dead."

"No, he isn't," Frank replied, and explained that they had found Rutlidge hiding out on Chapel Island under an assumed name.

Barnes's eyes widened as he listened to the story. "But why would he do that? It doesn't make sense."

Frank told Barnes about Rutlidge's plan to disprove the diamond's curse. "He felt that if he was still alive, he was legally the owner of the diamond. If his horse, Faith, won the race, obviously the curse did not work."

The detective shook his head. "Well, I sure would like to ask him some questions."

Dr. Werner interrupted the discussion. "I want to thank you again for all you've done," he said to the two boys who had saved his daughter. "Please let us repay you by inviting you to visit with us in our country soon."

The brothers thanked the geologist and told him they had been to Germany once before, but would love to go again.

The Rabbit, who had been listening to their words, let out a wild laugh. "In a few more minutes we will all be blown to bits," he spat. "When my bomb explodes, everything will come tumbling down."

The good humor disappeared from the faces in the group. Hearing the Rabbit's threat, Chet stood up from where he had been sitting on the beach. He looked at the high bluff wall that loomed overhead.

"Let's get out of here." He gulped, fearing that when the quake hit they would all be smothered by the cliffs tumbling down on top of them.

Jake had worries of his own. The quake could possibly cause a tidal wave of enough size in the bay to wipe out his birthplace, Chapel Island.

"Is it true what he's telling us?" Mr. Hardy asked the geologist.

"The bomb ought to have little or no effect," Dr. Werner replied, fixing his eyes on the terrorist.

The Rabbit's face went blank for a second before a sneer again formed his expression. "You have no idea how powerful it is," he said in a biting tone. "The one we set off in Bayport is nothing compared to this one."

"I took that into consideration," Werner answered evenly. "But the configuration of the earth below us ought to absorb nearly all of its impact."

The Rabbit struggled to kick the geologist, but Frank and Joe held him in place. "Believe what you will, Werner!" the Rabbit responded, his voice breaking into an eerie, high-pitched squeal. "But you will learn better very soon."

Although everyone thought the terrorist's threat was nothing more than a scare tactic, the mood of the success was broken. Katerina leaned silently against her father's shoulder. Sensing the change of spirit, the Doberman lay down with its head between its paws.

The somber mood lasted only a moment, however, before a thought occurred to Werner. He smiled. "I have something that you boys might be interested in." He proceeded to pace off steps on the ground, beginning with the spot where the hole had been bored. Counting twenty-five paces, he bent down and dug at the sand with his hands. In a moment he stood back up again, holding a jar. "Here," he said, unscrewing the lid and presenting the jar to Frank and Joe. Inside was a large gem, which twinkled as it caught the moonlight!

Joe's eyes lit up. "It's the Faith diamond!" he exclaimed. He poured the priceless gem into the palm of his hand and stared at it in wonder. "How did you get it?"

"I stole it from the Smithsonian," the geologist answered with a grin.

"So it wasn't Rutlidge after all!" Barnes exclaimed. "Boswell just thought it was."

Frank turned to Werner. "So you're the one who broke into the museum that night. Tell us about it."

The geologist chuckled. "Yes, I did. It was part of the plan I mentioned to you earlier."

"But why?" the older Hardy brother queried.

Werner cleared his throat and began to explain. "The diamond was to be the Rabbit's payment for his services. It was Jensen's job to get it for him. When I learned of this, I was determined to procure the gem myself and hold it until my daughter was released to me. That was the only way I could be sure of getting her back."

"So the Faith diamond was what the Rabbit and Roget were demanding from you the night we showed up at your bungalow." Joe put in.

"Yes," Werner said. "And it's a good thing you came. These men were much harder to deal with than I expected. They were prepared to beat it out of me."

The albino terrorist, now handcuffed and bound

186

by his feet, thrashed in the sand. "That's mine!" he shouted in anger, staring greedily at the gem.

Paying no attention to his rantings, Werner continued. "What I discovered was that Jensen had been trying to buy the stone from a man named Arthur Rutlidge."

Frank and Joe both wanted to interrupt at this point, but they restrained themselves.

"However, Rutlidge was not interested in the deal," Werner went on, "so Jensen tried less honest ways to make him sell. I believe the gem is reputed to bring misfortune to its owners, and Jensen contrived somehow to make it appear that the stone was affecting Rutlidge's horses."

Unable to contain themselves, the two sleuths told the story of how Max had used a dog whistle to cause the diamond owner's horses to lose races.

"We found Rutlidge hiding away on Chapel Island," Joe added. "He was supposed to have been drowned in a boating accident."

Werner raised his eyebrows in surprise at the youths' story. "You boys have certainly been doing a good job." He grinned. "That boating accident was my idea. But now I am getting ahead of myself. When Jensen's plan to make Rutlidge sell the diamond did not work, he began to threaten his life. That is when I made my move. I contacted Rutlidge. After convincing him that I was on his side, I told him to will his diamond to the museum, then to fake the boating accident. I arranged for him to take refuge on Chapel Island."

"And when the diamond ended up at the Smithsonian, you would steal it and hold it as collateral for your daughter," Frank added.

"It would also mean the stone still belonged to Rutlidge, but at the same time it would get Jensen off his back," Joe put in.

"Right." The geologist beamed. "It was a good deal all around."

"But if you were planning to trade the stone for Katerina," the dark-haired Hardy puzzled, "how was Rutlidge supposed to get his diamond back?"

Werner shrugged. "I hoped I would be able to get my daughter before I paid the Rabbit. But I would have gladly given him the gem if that had been necessary to insure Katerina's safety. Rutlidge agreed, by the way." The geologist then hugged his daughter gently and was silent.

Frank let a moment pass before speaking again. "I have only one more question, if you don't mind." He waited for Werner to nod before going on. "What was the purpose behind sabotaging the power plants?"

"Jensen represents some very shady oil merchants in the Mideast," Werner replied. "I suppose they wanted to discredit nuclear power by causing the quakes. Public opinion would then turn against nuclear energy and the price of oil would increase. But that's only a guess."

When the questioning was over, Katerina rewarded each of the boys with a kiss on the cheek. Chet blushed, having become attracted to the chestnut-haired girl. "Hey, let me take a look at that diamond," he said, trying to hide his embarrassment. He took the stone from Joe and held it up in the moonlight. "I bet this thing would pay for a lot of chocolate sundaes. I wonder how people ever got the idea it would bring bad luck. You'd have to be pretty superstitious to believe something like that."

Just then, a low rumble came from the earth. The ground began to tremble as the sound grew louder. Everyone froze for a moment.

"Here, take this thing back!" Chet cried, shoving the diamond into the geologist's hands.

"Quick, get on the yacht," Mr. Hardy ordered, worried the yellow clay would break off the bluff wall and bury the beach.

The group hastened to Jensen's cruiser, but by the time they were aboard, the trembling had stopped.

"Well, that was your earthquake," Werner told the Rabbit with a laugh. "Not much of a show for all the trouble you went to."

The terrorist growled, but did not reply.

Joe gave Chet a friendly slap on the back. "Now what were you saying about how stupid people were to believe in that diamond's powers?" he chided. "You sure were in a big hurry to get rid of it when the rumbling started."

"I was afraid I might drop it in the sand and it would get lost," Chet defended himself. "Of course I don't believe in that silly superstition."

No one knew at this point that Chet would soon have to worry about another superstition in *Track of the Zombie*.

Frank chuckled at his friend's excuse. "Okay, let's pack up our camping gear and head for Washington," he announced. "If we leave now, we'll make it back to Bayport in time for breakfast."

"Not so fast," the boys' father told them. "That skiff you sank is worth quite a bit of money. I'm afraid it will have to be paid for." Mr. Hardy watched his sons' faces pale as they realized their entire summer savings would be used up in paying for the skiff. "But since it was for a good cause," he added with a twinkle in his eye, "I'll cover it."

You are invited to join

THE OFFICIAL NANCY DREW ®/
HARDY BOYS ® FAN CLUB!

Be the first in your neighborhood to find out
about the newest adventures of Nancy, Frank,
and Joe in the **Nancy Drew** ®/ **Hardy Boys** ®
Mystery Reporter, and to receive your official
membership card. Just send your name, age,
address, and zip code on a postcard *only* to:

The Official Nancy Drew ®/
Hardy Boys ® **Fan Club**
Wanderer Books
Simon & Schuster Building
1230 Avenue of the Americas
New York, New York 10020

THE HARDY BOYS® SERIES
by Franklin W. Dixon

Night of the Werewolf (#59)
Mystery of the Samurai Sword (#60)
The Pentagon Spy (#61)
The Apeman's Secret (#62)
The Mummy Case (#63)
Mystery of Smugglers Cove (#64)
The Stone Idol (#65)
The Vanishing Thieves (#66)
The Outlaw's Silver (#67)
The Submarine Caper (#68)
The Four-Headed Dragon (#69)
The Infinity Clue (#70)

You will also enjoy

THE TOM SWIFT® SERIES
by Victor Appleton

The City in the Stars (#1)
Terror on the Moons of Jupiter (#2)
The Alien Probe (#3)
The War in Outer Space (#4)
The Astral Fortress (#5)
The Rescue Mission (#6)